RETURN TO ME

by
J. E. Terrall

ISBN: 978-0-9994727-7-4

This is a work of fiction. Names, characters, and incidents are either a product of the author's imagination or are used fictitiously, and any resemblance to actual persons, living or dead, is purely coincidental.

Printed in the United States of America
Third printing: 2017 by createspace.com

Cover designed by J.E. Terrall

* * * * * * *

"Listen," Sam said as he strained to hear and identify the strange sound.

Becky tried to listen. At first she could not hear anything unusual, but then she heard the faint sound of something off in the distance.

"What is it?" she asked.

"It sounds like some sort of engine."

Gradually, the sound became louder. Sam began to realize that it was an airplane engine that was sputtering and about to fail. Becky realized what it was at about the same time as Sam.

Suddenly, the sound of the engine stopped, it could no longer be heard at all. Sam looked at his daughter as she looked at him. They instantly knew what was about to happen. Becky stood up and stepped up beside her father as they listened.

"It's going to crash," Becky whispered.

* * * * * * *

Other Large Print Editions by J.E. Terrall

Western Short Stories
  The Old West
  The Frontier
  Untamed Land
  Tales from the Territory
  Frontier Justice

Western Novels
  Conflict in Elkhorn Valley
  The Valley Ranch War

Other Novels by J.E. Terrall
  Sing for Me
  Return to Me
  The Return Home

RETURN TO ME

To
Marilyn Robles,
my sister-in-law, for without her
I would not have met my wife.

CHAPTER ONE

It was shortly before noon when Matt Steward boarded his private twin engine airplane at the Richmond, Virginia, airport. His business meeting with Sky High Aviation Products of Richmond, had turned out much better than he had expected. In his briefcase he carried a contract that would save his small aviation parts company from bankruptcy. It would also allow him to continue in business for at least a few more years at a profit.

Before leaving Richmond, Virginia, he took a couple of minutes to call his office in Ohio and talk with his secretary, Julie. He told her of his success and she congratulated him. She suggested that she meet him at the airport when he arrived, and that they go out to dinner to celebrate. He agreed to dinner, but more to please her than for himself.

As Matt taxied his plane down the runway and it became airborne, he let his thoughts wander back over the past ten years and all the hard work he had put into his business. He had worked long hours each day, and most weekends, in his unrelenting drive to make his business a success. Julie had been his secretary for the past four years, as well as a good friend. She had been at his side through some of the hardest times.

Matt no longer heard the steady drone of the small airplane's engines as he flew west over the tree covered hills of Virginia. His mind was consumed with thoughts of his future and the future of his business.

Suddenly, without warning, there was a bright flash of light, a sharp crack and the loud, deafening sound of nearby thunder. It took a few seconds for his eyes to re-adjust from the flash of light. It was as if someone had shot off a flash bulb in his face, and all he could see were spots before his eyes for several seconds.

He had been so deep in thought that he had failed to notice the change in the weather. A quick look around made him acutely aware that he was flying directly into a dark, threatening thunderstorm. Not a good place for such a small airplane.

It had been slightly overcast when he took off from Richmond, but otherwise a fairly good day to fly. There had been no mention of severe thunderstorms in the forecast when he filed his flight plan, only reports of a few scattered light showers. However, he was aware that thunderstorms frequently pop up over the mountains that time of year, often with little or no warning.

The small airplane bounced around on the rapidly changing air currents. Matt held onto the wheel tightly in an effort to keep the airplane under control. He looked around for an opening in the clouds, or at least a place where the air currents might not be so rough. To the south, he thought he could see an area where the clouds did not seem to be as dark or as menacing.

He tried to turn the airplane south in the hope of flying it out of the storm and out of harm's way. The airplane was not responding very well to the controls as it was tossed around like a leaf in the wind.

There was a second flash of light and another loud crack of thunder as the airplane was suddenly hit by a bolt of lightning. The plane shook violently and the gauges twirled around out of control. Smoke began to seep out of the instrument panel and the radio squealed loudly in Matt's ears causing him to jerk the earphones off his head and toss them onto the seat beside him.

Matt could sense that he was rapidly losing what little control he had of the airplane. He knew that he had veered way off course. His attention was drawn to one of the engines as it was beginning to sputter and chock. Looking out the side window, he saw the engine suddenly quit.

Dark streaks of oil crept out from under the engine's cowling. He quickly cut fuel to the engine and feathered the propeller in an effort to reduce drag against the airplane. He let out a sigh of relief that the engine had not caught on fire, but he still knew that he was not out of trouble.

According to the write-ups on the airplane, it was supposed to be able to fly on one engine. Matt doubted it could fly on one engine in the kind of weather he was experiencing. Even though the gauges were no longer working and he could not see the ground, he could tell that the airplane was gradually losing altitude. He opened the throttle in an effort to increase the rpm's to the remaining engine, but the engine did not respond. Without the increased rpm's the airplane was sure to go down.

Without his radio, he had no way to tell anyone that he was going to crash. Even if he could tell someone, he had no idea of his exact location. Glancing at his watch and estimating the time he had been in the air, he guessed that he was somewhere close to the West Virginia State line over the Allegheny Mountains.

He strained to see out the window in the hope of seeing some place where he could try to set the airplane down. He hoped for a glimpse of a road, an open field, or any place that would provide a reasonable landing site. His visibility was limited to only a few hundred feet at best. All he could see were dark gray clouds and streaks of rainwater flowing over the windshield. He had no idea how far above the trees or the ground he might be.

The remaining engine began to sputter and cough. Suddenly, the remaining engine gave a final sputter and died. The vibrations and the sounds of the engines were gone. The only sounds were those of the wind rushing past the airplane, and of the raindrops splattering against the windshield.

Matt feathered the propeller. He knew that a crash landing in the mountainous area like the Alleghenies could mean a very long wait before anyone might find him. It would not be the first time that the Allegheny Mountains had swallowed up a small airplane like his.

He pulled his seat belt tighter in an effort to prepare himself for a very rough landing. Taking a firm grip on the wheel, he continued to watch out the windshield and the side window hoping, praying, for a clear spot to appear in the midst of the clouds and the mist that shrouded him in darkness.

Suddenly, the tops of trees appeared directly in front of him. He pulled back on the wheel as he tried to pull the nose of the airplane up. The nose came up only slightly, but it was too late. The airplane began crashing through the trees. The wings began cutting off the tops of trees and tearing off branches as the airplane plowed through them.

As the plane dropped lower and lower, the branches of the trees grow bigger and bigger. The only sounds Matt could hear were the deafening sounds of branches hitting the airplane and the tearing of sheet metal as the airplane started to break apart. Tree branches slapped against the windshield as tree trunks ripped at the airplane's thin metal skin and tore off pieces of the wings and tail section.

The last thing Matt saw as the airplane bounced and twisted its way through the trees was a large branch as it smashed through the windshield. He felt a sharp pain in his head and bright flashes of light in front of his eyes, then everything went blank.

* * * *

The large old stone house, built before the Civil War, sat back near the edge of the woods. The small garden beside the house was thick with corn, peas, tomatoes and other vegetables growing in the rich mountain soil. Across the lawn was a big old stone barn with several paddocks along the sides and across the back. On the other side of the lane was a large pasture of lush, thick, green grass surrounded by a white board fence.

The rain poured down off the porch roof and onto the ground. The rainwater flowed down the lane making it very muddy while cutting deep groves in what had been shallow wheel ruts. It had been raining off and on for the past several days, but today the downpour had continued for several hours.

Becky McCullen sat on the porch swing with her feet tucked under her. It was a little chilly and damp that morning. She pulled the heavy hand-knitted sweater tightly around herself in an effort to keep warm. The only sounds were the steady patter of the rain on the roof and the splashing of the water on the ground as it fell from the edge of the porch roof. There was also the occasional sound of thunder off in the distance. She watched the rain as she slowly moved back and forth on the porch swing.

Sam McCullen stepped through the doorway and out onto the porch. Leaning against the wall, he looked at the young woman and smiled.

"You warm enough, honey? I have a nice fire going inside."

"I'm fine, Daddy."

"I sure do like the smell of a fresh rain, don't you?"

"Yes. It's like everything is being washed clean. Except this rain will not only wash everything clean, it will probably wash everything away if it doesn't end soon," she replied.

"The weather report says it should clear some tomorrow," Sam commented.

"By the way, how's the mare doing?" he added.

"She's doing much better. I'll go change the dressing on her neck after lunch. The wound is still open and draining a little. The cuts on her side are healing very well."

"Good," Sam replied with a nod of approval.

"I understand that Billy Joe and his father went after the cat that attacked the mare. Have you heard from them?" she asked.

"I haven't heard anything yet. I seriously doubt they found it in this weather."

Becky looked out over her father's farm. It was so peaceful here. She liked to come home whenever she could, which did not seem to be often enough. Now that she had been laid off from work, she could spend a little time on the farm before she started looking for a new job.

Sam moved out of the doorway, stepping out onto the porch and up to the railing. He leaned on it as he looked out over the pasture. It was easy to tell that he had something on his mind, but he was not sure how to approach the subject.

"Honey, does Billy Joe know that you're home?" he asked without turning around to face her.

It was the very subject that Becky had hoped to avoid. She knew how much her father seemed to like Billy Joe. In fact, she liked him, too. She just was not sure if she loved him, or if her feelings for him had sort of melted away with time. In any case, she did not want to talk about him right now.

"I don't think so," she said with a sigh.

"Don't you think that you should tell him you're home?"

"I will," she assured her father.

Becky and Billy Joe had been dating off and on for some time. Billy Joe was in love with her, and she knew it. It was hard enough for her to explain how she felt about him to herself without having to try to explain her feelings to her father. She had hoped that he would not bring up the subject at all, even though she knew she would not be able to avoid it forever.

"Listen," Sam said as he strained to hear and identify the strange sound.

Becky tried to listen. At first she could not hear anything unusual, but then she heard the faint sound of something off in the distance.

"What is it?" she asked.

"It sounds like some sort of engine."

Gradually, the sound became louder. Sam began to realize that it was an airplane engine that was sputtering and about to fail. Becky realized what it was at about the same time as her father.

Suddenly, the sound of the engine stopped, it could no longer be heard at all. Sam looked at his daughter as she looked at him. They instantly knew what was about to happen. Becky stood up and stepped up beside her father as they listened.

"It's going to crash," Becky whispered.

"Sssssssssh."

Sam listened very carefully, straining in an effort to hear the airplane crash. If he was lucky, very lucky, he might be able to get some kind of bearing on where it went down. Certainly, whoever was in the airplane would need help if the crash did not kill them outright.

They thought they heard the sound of something in the woods, possibly the airplane crashing through the trees up on the ridge behind the house. It was not very far away, but it would be difficult for them to get up there.

"Call the sheriff and tell him that a plane went down on the ridge. I'll get the first aid kit."

Becky ran into the house. She picked up the receiver and listened for a dial tone, but the phone was dead. She clicked the receiver several times in an effort to get a dial tone, but nothing.

"The phone's dead," Becky called out to her father.

"The road is probably washed out, too," he said as he came into the living room with the first aid kit in his hand.

"We'll just have to find the plane ourselves, and do what we can for whoever is still alive," Becky said as she hung up the phone.

"Get your boots and raincoat," Sam said as he headed for the back door where he kept his boots and raincoat.

Becky followed him out onto the screened-in back porch. She put on her boots, then took her raincoat off the hook and put it on. Sam handed the first aid kit to her while he slipped into his boots and raincoat.

As soon as they were ready, they started off the back porch and into the woods. They knew it would not be an easy trek to get to the top of the ridge. Even after they reached the ridge, there would be the difficulty of finding the downed airplane.

But no matter how difficult it was, they still had to do whatever they could. They had to at least try. After all, they were most likely the only people who were aware that an airplane had crashed.

CHAPTER TWO

The past few days of rain had saturated the ground making it very muddy. Even the rocks were slippery, making the going very difficult for Sam and Becky. Several times during their climb up the ridge they lost their footing and fell on the steep slopes. At one point, Sam fell, sliding almost twenty feet back down a steep embankment causing him to drop the first aid kit. The wet ground had given way and slid out from under him feet. Fortunately, he was not injured. However, he lost the first aid kit somewhere in the mud. They decide to continue on without it as it would take too long to find it.

Sam was familiar with the area and knew of a place where some rocks stuck out overlooking a large part of the western slope of the ridge. It had taken them almost two hours just to get to the outcropping and they still had to find the airplane. Becky waited at the base of the outcropping while her father worked his way up to the top.

When Sam reached the top, he looked back down the hillside toward the farm and the valley below. It was difficult to see anything with the rain and the mist hanging over the valley. Sam looked up and down the valley in the hope of seeing something that would give him a clue where the airplane might be found.

"Can you see anything?" Becky called from below.

"No," he answered as he continued to look around.

Just as he was about to give up and climb down off the rock, he noticed something in the trees several hundred feet below and to the right of him. He could not make out what it was, but it did not seem to belong up there. It appeared to be shiny, or light colored, and stuck almost straight up in the air. He was sure that it was not a rock. He could not think of anything that would look like that up there.

"I can see something down there," he yelled down to Becky as he pointed toward it.

"Is it an airplane?" Becky called back to him.

"Can't say for sure, but I don't remember ever seeing anything like it from up here before."

Becky waited impatiently for her father to climb back down. Together, they worked their way around the base of the rock and along the side of the hill. It was another half an hour or more before they were able to work their way through the thick woods to where they discovered part of the tail rudder of a small airplane sticking straight up in the air.

"I think this is what I saw from the ridge," Sam commented as he looked at the piece of metal dangling from the tree.

"Look! The plane must have gone through here." Becky pointed down the steep hill where a swath had been recently cut through trees.

They followed the path for only a few hundred feet before they came upon the remains of a small airplane. The wings had been completely torn off the fuselage, and were littered along the path the airplane had taken. The fuselage had been ripped open along the bottom and sides. There were pieces of metal along with parts of the interior spread all over the ground. The tree's branches had smashed out most of the windows of the small aircraft.

Sam looked at the remains of the airplane and wondered if anyone could have survived such a crash. Becky climbed over several fallen trees as she tried to get to the cockpit of the airplane. As she stepped up to the cockpit and looked inside, she saw the pilot.

"Over here!" she called out to her father.

Becky looked at the man in the pilot's seat. He was slumped forward over the steering wheel and he was not moving. She could not see his face, but she could see blood mixed with rain, small branches and dirt in his hair and inside the cabin. There were streaks of blood on the side of his face and down his neck. She was not sure if he was still alive.

Almost afraid of what she would discover, she slowly reached in through the broken outside window and pressed the ends of her fingers to his neck. It took her a few seconds, but she found a faint pulse.

"He's alive! He's still alive!" she called out.

Sam took a quick look at what was left of the airplane as he tried to figure out how to get the pilot out of it. He discovered that the door was on the other side. As quickly as possible, he climbed over the rubble to get to the other side of the airplane. As he came around to the other side, he noticed a little smoke and small flashes of light coming from under the fuselage. He was sure that an electrical short caused the sparks. He could also smell the odor of airplane fuel.

"We have to get him out. This thing could go up in flames at anytime," Sam called out.

Sam stepped up on the stubby remains of a wing, grabbed the edge of the door and pulled. The frame was twisted and the door would not budge. He jerked and pulled on the door again and again. Finally, the door gave way and swung open causing Sam to lose his footing and fall to the ground. Unhurt, he quickly got up and climbed into the airplane. After crawling across the cabin, he unhooked the pilot's seat belt and he began dragging him toward the door. The injured pilot had to be removed from the plane, and quickly.

Becky quickly got around to the other side of the airplane and was waiting at the door to help her father. Sam pulled the pilot across the seats and out of the airplane. There was no time to worry about causing more injuries to the pilot. They had to get him out before the plane when up in flames.

Once he had the pilot out, Becky grabbed his feet and helped her father carry him away from the airplane. They needed to get him away from the airplane before the sparks ignited the fuel.

Together, they carried the pilot away from the wreckage of the plane. The ground was slippery and their footing was bad. Becky slipped in the mud causing her to drop the pilot's feet as she fell. Sam fell at the same time, dropping him to the ground.

Suddenly, there was a loud whooshing sound from near the airplane. Becky turned and looked back toward the airplane to see it completely engulfed in flames. Even with the cold rain in her face, she could feel the intense heat from the fire as the thought of what could have happened had they not gotten the pilot out when they did.

Sam sat on the cold wet ground and watched as the airplane burned while he tried to catch his breath. He was relieved that there had not been anyone else in the airplane and that it had not exploded.

Looking around at the trees, Sam knew that there was little chance the fire would spread and start a forest fire as the woods were soaking wet from all the rain over the past few days. Once the fuel burned up, he was sure the fire would simply go out.

Becky looked over at her father, then at the pilot. She crawled up beside him and wiped some of the mud and dirt from his face. It was the first time that she had gotten a good look at him. Even with all the blood and mud, she could see that he was a handsome man.

He was still unconscious when she checked his pulse again. She wondered who he was, where he had come from and where he was going.

"We better get him to the house," Sam said interrupting Becky's thoughts.

"How are we going to get him back? It took us two hours just to get up here. I'm not sure he will last that long."

Sam could hear the deep concern and frustration in his daughter's voice. He was as concerned for the young pilot as she was, and she did have a good point.

"We don't have much choice. We have to get him to the house, and we certainly can't carry him that far. We'll have to put him inside my raincoat and drag him down the hill. It will be slow going, but I don't have a better idea," Sam said.

Becky nodded her head in agreement. She realized that there was little choice. Reaching down, she wrapped her arms around the pilot's neck and lifted him up to a sitting position while her father took off his raincoat.

Sam opened his coat and put the pilot's arms in the sleeves. Becky laid the pilot back down on the raincoat and buttoned the coat over him. Sam reached down and grabbed hold of the collar. He looked up at his daughter to see if she was ready, then started to pull, dragging the pilot along behind him.

It was hard work, but not as hard as Sam had expected. The rain had turned the ground to mud and most of it was down hill. The mud was slippery and made it difficult for Sam to keep his footing. Becky walked along side and watched the pilot as they moved toward the house.

Sam stopped every once in awhile so that Becky could check on the pilot, and so he could take a short break. Becky would check the pilot's pulse and feel his head. He seemed to be hanging on pretty well, but Becky knew that he would not be able to survive if they did not get him someplace warm and dry soon.

It seemed like it had taken forever to get to the house, but once in the house they laid him on an old quilt in front of the fire place. Sam built up the fire while Becky gathered up some blankets to put over the pilot.

While kneeling beside the fireplace, Sam looked over at his daughter. She had gotten a pan of water and was washing off the pilot's face.

Once the fire had warmed the room, they removed his wet and muddy clothes. Sam helped Becky examine the pilot for wounds and broken bones as they bathed him. They had not had time to examine him for any broken bones up on the mountain. The only open wound they found, other than some minor scratches, was on his head. Becky bandaged the wound while Sam wrapped the pilot in the blankets, trying to make him as comfortable as possible.

"There's nothing else we can do for him now, except wait," Sam said as he sat down next to the fireplace. "Why don't you go take a shower? I'll stay with him."

"You take your shower first," she suggested.

Sam decided that he would not argue with her. He was tired, wet and in need of a shower. Standing up, he stretched his stiff and tired muscles. Looking down at the pilot, Sam wondered if the man would survive. There was little they could do for him other than keep him dry and warm. It was going to be nip and tuck for awhile, and only time would tell.

Becky sat at the pilot's side watching him. He was so close to death, and there was little she could do for him except to make him as comfortable as possible. She listened to him breath and checked his pulse often.

Without realizing it, she found herself simply holding his hand. She did not know if it helped him or not, but it made her feel a little better.

Looking down at him, she wondered what he had been doing flying around in such bad weather in such a small airplane. She checked his hand for a ring, but there was no ring. Again, she wondered who the man was.

After tucking his hand under the covers, she got up and moved over by the fireplace where his clothes were piled. She searched through his pockets for something that might identify him, but found nothing except a short note that made no sense to her. There was no wallet, no credit cards, and no driver's license, nothing that would tell her who he was. The shirt he had been wearing was a rather expensive shirt. The pants were of a good quality material and were apparently suit pants. She concluded that he must have had his coat off and that it was still in the airplane. If he carried his wallet in his coat like a lot of businessmen did, it would have been destroyed when the airplane went up in flames.

Becky sat there on the hearth with her elbows on her knees and her chin in her hands as she looked down at the man lying on the floor in front of her. His clothes had given her no clue as to who he might be. The only thing she knew about him was that he was handsome, probably in his early thirties, in very good physical shape and that he was a pilot. She was also relatively certain that his chances of surviving without medical care were not very good.

"How's he doing," Sam said as he entered the room.

Becky turned and looked at her father.

"Nothing's changed."

"Why don't you go ahead and take your shower. I'll watch him."

"I have to change the dressing on the mare."

"Okay. Change the dressing on the mare, then take a shower. I'll fix us something to eat."

Becky looked from her father to the man lying quietly on the quilt. Sam could see the worried look on Becky's face.

"He is resting well. It is best if you just let him rest. I'll check on him every few minutes," he promised.

Becky turned to look at her father and forced a smile. He had always been able to tell what was on her mind just by looking at her.

"Okay," she conceded. "I'll take care of all the horses while I'm out."

Becky stood up and went out to the back porch. She slipped into her raincoat and boots again, then walked out to the barn. After checking the mare and changing the dressing, she made sure the rest of the horses were fed and bedded down for the night.

When she was finished, Becky returned to the house. Leaving her boots and raincoat on the back porch, she entered the kitchen. She could smell dinner cooking. It smelled delicious and for the first time she realized that she was hungry. She had not eaten since early morning.

"How's he doing?" she asked.

"No change. Go take your shower."

"What's for dinner?"

"A big bowl of my hot beef stew, one of your favorites. It'll be ready by the time you finish showering."

Becky gave her father a quick kiss on the cheek, then went upstairs to her bedroom. She stripped out of her clothes, dumped them in the hamper and went into her bathroom. Turning on the water, she knew that with the power off the water would be lukewarm at best. She stepped into the shower and shivered as the tepid water flowed over the smooth lines of her body.

She quickly washed her hair and rinsed the soap from it. Her long dark hair flowed down her back well below her shoulders. After washing herself, she rinsed off and stepped out of the shower. She rubbed herself briskly with a towel to help keep the chill off, then wrapped a smaller towel around her head. Taking her long velvet robe from the behind the door, she slipped into it and tied it tightly around her narrow waist. After stepping into a warm pair of slippers, she went back downstairs.

Becky went directly to the living room to check on the pilot. After checking his pulse, she sat down in a chair and watched him. She looked up as her father came into the room.

"Ready to eat?"

"Sure," she replied as she stood up.

Becky followed her father to the kitchen and sat down at the table. They sat quietly while they ate. It had been a long day for both of them and they were tired. As soon as Becky had finished her stew, she looked over at her father. He was getting up in years. The trek into the mountains to rescue the pilot had been hard on him. He needed a good night's sleep.

"I'm going to sleep down here."

Becky had already decided that she would sleep in the living room so that she could be close to the pilot just in case he woke up during the night.

"I kind of figured you would. Call me if you need me."

"I will."

"I tried to make a call, but the lines are still down. The radio said there has been a lot of flooding in the area so I doubt we could get him to the hospital. We'll just have to do what we can for him, and hope for the best."

Becky knew what it was like to be cut off from the rest of the world for days at a time. It was not the first time that the roads had been washed out and the telephone lines down due to storms. The farm was at least six miles from the nearest paved road and another twenty-four or more miles to the nearest hospital, and that was just a small country hospital.

Sam cleared the table while Becky fixed herself a place to sleep on the sofa. She lay down on the sofa and pulled the covers over her. She rolled over on her side so she could keep an eye on the pilot.

After a short time, Sam came into the living room to check on them. He put another couple of logs on the fire, kissed Becky on the forehead and went upstairs to bed. Becky lay there watching the man until she dozed off.

CHAPTER THREE

Becky woke early in the morning to the sharp crack of lightning and the loud rumble of thunder. The weather had not cleared. It was still raining, although it had slowed to little more than a steady drizzle. The air was still chilly and damp. The fire had burned down to embers and the living room had a slight chill to it.

Becky rolled over and looked at the man lying in front of the fireplace. She immediately noticed that he must have moved a little during the night. Sitting up, she reached down and pulled the covers back up over his shoulders. Since she was up, she decided to put some wood on the fire before it went completely out.

Wrapping her blanket over her shoulders and pulling it around herself, she moved around the pilot to the hearth and picked up a couple of small logs. After placing the logs on the fire, she sat down on the hearth and waited for the logs to start burning. The logs quickly burst into flames spreading their heat into the room.

Becky noticed the man seemed to be breathing more easily, and a little color had returned to his face. Becky wondered if he woke up last night or if he had simply rolled over in his sleep. She also wondered how long it would be before he would wake up so she could talk to him. It was clear that there was nothing she could do, except wait.

Becky stood up and went out to the kitchen. With the power to the house still out, she was glad that her father had kept the old gas stove. She was looking around for something to fix for breakfast when her father came into the kitchen.

"Morning, honey," he said.

"Good morning."

"How's your patient doing?"

"All right, I guess. He still hasn't come around, but his color's better."

"That's a good sign. How about if I fix breakfast?"

"Great. I'll go get dressed."

Becky kissed her father on the cheek as she passed him and went upstairs to her bedroom. She picked out a pair of jeans and a white blouse from her closet. With the chill in the air, she thought that a sweatshirt would be a good idea, too. As soon as she was dressed and combed her hair, she returned to the kitchen.

"What are you going to do, today?" Sam asked.

"I figured I'd take care of the horses and keep an eye on our patient."

"I've got a couple of things to do out in the barn, so why don't I take care of the horses. There's no need for both of us going out in the rain," Sam said as he set two plates on the table.

Becky nodded her approval of her father's suggestion as she looked at the bacon and scrambled eggs he had prepared for her. She sat down at the table and watched Sam as he poured each of them a cup of coffee then sat down across the table from her. Becky hesitated to eat while Sam dug right in.

"What's the matter, honey?" Sam asked.

"I was just thinking."

"About what?"

"I wonder if he has a family somewhere. If he does, they're probably worried about him."

"I'm sure they are, but there's nothing we can do about it right now."

"I know. I was just wondering."

"You better eat up before your eggs get cold."

Becky smiled at her father and started to eat. She knew he was right, as usual. He had always told her to try not to worry about those things she could not do anything about. It was just was one of those things.

Sam finished his breakfast, stood up and took his dishes to the sink. He drank down the last of his coffee before putting the cup on the counter, then went out on the back porch to get his boots and raincoat.

"Be careful out there," Becky said.

"I will. Keep the coffee hot."

"I will," she said with a smile as she watched him step off the back porch and go out into the rain.

Becky watched her father as he walked across the yard and headed toward the barn. As soon as he was out of sight, she turned around and went back into the kitchen.

As she began washing the breakfast dishes, she looked out the window. It was still raining and a mist hung over the ridge where the airplane had crashed. Looking up toward the ridge made her think about the pilot. She turned and looked toward the living room as her mind filled with questions. Where could he have been going that was so important he would fly in the kind of weather they had yesterday, she wondered. What could have been so important that a man would risk his life like that? Of course, there were no answers to her questions, at least not until he could answer them for her.

Becky finished the dishes, poured herself a cup of coffee and took it into the living room. She sat down in an easy chair next to the window, picked up the book she had been reading, and made herself as comfortable as possible.

At first, she would glance over her book to check on the pilot every few minutes. He looked the same each time she checked on him. He was breathing well and his color was good, but he lay motionless on the quilt. There was nothing more she could do for him. She would just have to wait until he came around, and it could be a very long wait. Gradually, she became engrossed in her book and no longer glanced over at him every few minutes.

Becky did not realize how much time had gone by when she again looked over the top of her book at the pilot. At first glance, she didn't notice any change in him. She did not notice that his eyes were open and that he was looking back at her. She turned her attention back at her book and started to read again. She almost dropped the book when it registered in her mind that he was awake and watching her.

"Hello," Becky said as she closed her book.

For some reason her greeting sounded a little strange, but she did not know what else to say. She set her book on the end table next to the sofa, then stood up. She walked over to the fireplace and sat down on the hearth next to him.

Matt did not say anything. He lay still, but looked around by moving only his eyes. The surroundings were not familiar to him. The only thing Matt was absolutely sure of was that he had a splitting headache.

Matt turned his head slightly to get a better look at the woman sitting next to him. She did not look like anyone that he knew, although he liked what he saw. The snug fitting jeans and the comfortable looking sweatshirt looked very nice on the complete stranger. She had a pretty face and pleasant smile framed with long dark hair.

"Who are you?" he asked in a quiet voice.

"I'm Rebecca McCullen, but my friends call me Becky. Who are you?"

"I'm, ah, -- ah."

Matt was sure he had a name, but what was it? He tried to search his mind in an effort to remember who he was, but no matter how hard he tried, he could not come up with a name, any name.

"I'm not sure," he conceded.

Becky could see the confused look on his face. She wondered what could be wrong with him that he could not remember his own name. All she could think of was that he must have taken a harder bump on the head than they thought.

"Do you remember your name?" she asked quietly, trying not to cause him any more stress.

Matt thought for a minute, but he could not think of his name. In fact, he could not remember anything.

"No," he replied in a whisper.

"You took a pretty nasty bump on the head. I wouldn't worry about it. It will come to you."

Becky was trying very hard to reassure him that everything would be fine, but she was worried, too.

"What happened?"

Becky told him about the crash of his airplane on the ridge, and how they had brought him down off the mountain. She told him about the airplane burning and everything that was in it was destroyed. She even apologized for not being able to save any of his things.

As she explained what happened as best she could figure it, Matt tried to remember. He could not remember flying an airplane, the storm yesterday, the crash on the mountain, the trip down the mountain, or anything else that seemed to matter. The harder he tried, the more his head seemed to hurt. He turned his head away from Becky and let out a long sigh of disappointment.

Becky wanted to help him, but she had no idea what she could do for him. It was clear that he had a headache, but there was much more to it than that.

"Would you like some aspirin?" she asked.

"What?" he asked turning back to look at her again.

"Would you like some aspirin for your headache?"

"Ah, yes, please."

Becky stood up and went out to the kitchen. She got the aspirin out of the cupboard and a glass of water, then returned to the living room. As she knelt down beside him, he tried to sit up, but he quickly discovered how sore and stiff he was from the accident. He groaned with pain.

Becky held his head as he took the aspirin and sipped some of the water. She gently laid his head back down on the pillow.

"Close your eyes and relax for a little while. Give the aspirin a chance to work. Rest is the best thing for you, right now. We can talk later, when you're feeling better," she suggested.

Matt closed his eyes and tried to relax, but it was difficult. He was trying to remember what happened in his life yesterday, the day before, or anytime for that matter; but he could not remember a thing.

Gradually, he was beginning to feel several aches and pains over most of his body. He was thinking that she must have been telling him the truth. He must have been in some kind of an accident to hurt so much. Maybe, the woman was right. Maybe, he had crashed an airplane, but he could not remember flying, let alone being a pilot like she said.

He heard movement near him and opened his eyes. He watched Becky move around and kneel down above his head. She leaned forward and put her hands on the sides of his head. Slowly, she made small circular movements with her fingers on his temples.

The gentle massage felt good and helped him to relax. He watched her for a minute or so, then closed his eyes again. Matt could feel the pain in his head slowly go away. It was so relaxing that he decided to let himself drift off into a restful sleep. He could try to figure out what was going on later.

Becky gently massaged his temples until she was sure he was asleep again. She hoped that the next time he woke up, he might remember his name. If not, at least he might feel a little better. She sat back on her heels and looked down at him.

The bruises and the cut on his head would soon heal; the black and blue marks on his arms and chest would be sore, but they, too, would heal. He would get better and then he would leave, that was to be expected. Why did that thought bother her so much?

Becky stood up and went out to the kitchen to get some more coffee. She stopped and looked out the window. It was not the woods or the rain that filled her thoughts, but rather the man sleeping in front of the fireplace. What must he be thinking if he could not remember his own name?

Becky was so deep in thought that she did not hear her father come back into the house. When he dropped his boots on the back porch, it startled her, and she turned to see him enter the kitchen.

"How's he doing?" Sam asked, not realizing that he had disturbed Becky's thoughts.

"He was awake for a little while. He seems to be coherent, but he can't remember his name," Becky said.

Sam could sense the concern and the worry in Becky's voice.

"I wouldn't worry too much about it, he took a pretty nasty hit on the head. He's bound to have some memory loss, but it will most likely be temporary. With some rest and a little time, he should be okay."

Becky trusted her father's judgment, and it gave her some comfort to think that he was probably right. She smiled and poured him a cup of coffee. After handing him the cup, she picked up her cup. They sat down at the table together.

"How's the mare doing?" she asked in an effort to get her mind off of the man sleeping on the living room floor.

"She looks pretty good this morning. The dressing you put on yesterday seems to be dry. I think the wound has stopped draining."

"Is she eating?"

"Like a horse," he said with a smile.

Becky laughed. She had always enjoyed spending time with her father. Being in the city and away from home so much, made these times even more pleasant for her.

Sam glanced out the window. "I sure hope this rain stops pretty soon. The lane is washing out in some places."

"Did you feed all the horses?"

"Sure did. That horse of yours is getting restless to get out. As long as there's lightening about, I think he should stay in the barn."

"You're probably right. Maybe, I can get him out later this afternoon."

Sam and Becky sipped their coffee and enjoyed some more casual conversation. They had not enjoyed each other's company for some time. Gradually, the conversation came back around to the man in the next room.

"You suppose he might be a government official?" Sam asked.

"What makes you think that?"

"I don't know. He was flying a plane, his suit was fairly expensive and he's clean shaven."

"That could fit almost anyone. The plane was very much like those a lot of businessmen use these days. He was probably on a business trip and ran into bad weather," Becky surmised.

Becky's thoughts drifted to the man and what he might do for a living. Gradually, her thoughts turned to another question that kept creeping into Becky's mind. It was not the first time that she had asked herself if he is married.

"Maybe, we should go in and check on him?" Becky suggested.

"You go ahead. I want to get a little more coffee. I'll be along in a minute."

Becky stood up and went into the living room while Sam went over to the stove to refill his cup. His concerns were for his daughter. She had always been the one to look out for strays and injured animals, but she always seemed to get attached to them. He thought for a second that she might get attached to the man; but he shook his head and reminded himself that it was a man not some stray animal. Taking his cup of coffee, he turned and went into the living room.

CHAPTER FOUR

When Becky returned to the living room, Matt was leaning against the mantel above the fireplace gazing down into the fire. He had the blanket wrapped loosely around his shoulders. He was breathing hard. In his effort to stand, he had used most of his strength and was feeling very weak and very confused.

Becky immediately noticed that he was beginning to sway back and forth a little. He looked as if he was about to lose his balance and fall. She rushed to his side, wrapped her arms around him for support and helped him regain his balance. Afraid that she might not be able to hold him if his legs buckled and he started to fall, she lowered him so that he could sit on the hearth.

"What are you doing?" she asked.

He looked at her. His eyes filled with confusion.

"I have to go," he said in a whisper.

"Go where?"

Becky felt a spark of hope that he was beginning to remember, but the spark was quickly smothered by the puzzled and confused look on his face. It was all she needed to see in order to know that he did not know where he was, let alone where he wanted to go. She felt powerless to help him. Even though it was not possible for her to understand what it must be like not to be able to remember even the simplest of things, she had to try to understand.

"Where is it that you have to go?"

"I don't know," he replied as he turned and looked into her eyes.

Something in the back of his mind had told him that he had been going somewhere, but he could not think of where, or even why. It seemed the harder he tried to think, the more lost and confused he became.

"How would you like to sit in a chair for awhile?" Becky asked.

"Do I have any clothes?" he asked.

It was a simple question, but it surprised Becky. She had not even thought about his need for clothes. The clothes he had been wearing when they found him were ruined. His question made her wonder if she had subconsciously not expected him to survive.

"I'll get you something to wear. Wait right here."

Becky looked over at her father who was standing in the doorway watching the two of them. She did not know how long he had been there, but she wanted him to do something. Either go get something for the pilot to wear, or sit with him while she got him something.

"I think I have some pants that he could wear, and a sweatshirt," Sam said thoughtfully. "I'll be right back."

Sam took a sip of his coffee, set the cup on a nearby table, then turned and went upstairs while Becky sat with the pilot. Sam was sure that he would be able to wear his pants, and that a baggy sweatshirt would work, too. He returned in a few minutes with clothes for him.

Becky went into the kitchen while Sam helped Matt get dressed. It took them awhile as he was very weak, as well as stiff and sore. It was hard for him to raise his arms up and slip the sweatshirt over his head, but with Sam's help he managed.

"You can come back. We're ready for company," Sam called out to Becky.

Becky returned to the living room to find her father sitting on the hearth, and the man sitting in Sam's big easy chair next to the fireplace. Matt had a blanket wrapped around his legs.

"You look much better. How do you feel?" Becky asked as she sat down on the sofa.

"Okay, I guess. Well, my head hurts, but not as much as it did earlier."

"Do you hurt anywhere else?"

"My chest hurts, and my right arm and shoulder," he added.

"I'm not surprised. You're a very lucky man," Sam said.

"What happened to me?"

"You were in an airplane crash up on the ridge behind our house. You are very lucky to even be alive. The plane went up in flames shortly after we pulled you out," Sam explained to him.

"Do you remember anything?" Becky asked.

Matt looked down at the floor as he tried to think. He could not seem to remember anything, anything at all. As he tried to think, there was a flash of the face of someone in his head. It was so quick he hardly had time to notice it. The instant vision startled him.

Becky noticed that he had flinched suddenly. She wondered if he was having some pain, or if he possibly remembered something.

"What's the matter? Are you all right?"

"I don't know. I think I got just a glimpse of someone, but I'm not sure," he said as he looked at Becky.

His brief encounter with a strange face confused Matt even more. Becky thought that he suddenly looked very tired, as if what he had seen had instantly drained him of what little strength he had left. She knew he needed to rest if he was going to get better.

"Why don't you lean back and take a nap. We can talk again later," Becky suggested, unable to hide her deep concern for him.

Matt did not hesitate. He tipped his head back and closed his eyes. He wanted sleep to come quickly, but sleep took its time. His mind was working to search his memory in an effort to find his past. No matter how hard he tried, he could not remember anything. Finally, he was able to let himself relax enough to doze off.

Becky sat in a chair several feet away from him. She wondered what was going on in his head. For several minutes, she watched him try to go back to sleep. Although he did not move very much, she could sense that he was having difficulty getting any real rest.

Gradually, Matt's breathing became deeper and slower, with the smooth evenness of someone who was sleeping. Reassured that he was resting, Becky picked up the book she had been reading and opened it to the place where she had left off. She started to read again, but found her mind continually returning to the young pilot. Concentration on the book was simply out of the question.

Setting the book back down on the table, she curled her legs under herself as she watched him sleep. Who was the man? Where did he come from? What was he like? Was he married and did he have a family? One question after another came rushing through her mind again and again, but they were questions that would have to wait to be answered.

Becky was so deep in concentration that she jumped when her father came up beside her, reached out and touched her on the shoulder. She turned and looked up at him.

"Are you okay, honey?"

"I'm fine, Daddy," she replied with a reassuring smile.

"It stopped raining."

Becky looked out the window. Sure enough the rain had stopped. The sun was not shining yet, but it would probably come out by afternoon.

"I'll let the horses out after lunch. They have been cooped up long enough," she said.

"So have you. You need to get outside, too."

"But we can't leave him alone."

"I'll watch him," Sam reassured her.

"Who do you think he is?" Becky asked looking back over toward Matt.

"I don't know, honey."

Although Sam responded to her question, he knew that she was only thinking out loud. It was most likely going to be awhile before they would be able to find out anything about him. It would be a couple of days before the road would be passable, and at least that long before they would have phone service again so that they could notify the sheriff that he was there.

Sam walked over to the fireplace and put another log on the fire. After glancing at the sleeping man, he went out to the kitchen, poured himself a cup of coffee and sat down at the kitchen table to read his weekly paper he had not bothered to look at since it arrived several days ago.

Becky watched the man sleep for several minutes before leaning back and closing her eyes. She did not go right to sleep, but it did not take long before she dozed off.

* * * *

Matt woke and looked around the room. It looked just the same as it had when he closed his eyes earlier. It was not a dream after all. He had hoped that it might look different somehow, maybe more familiar. As his eyes slowly scanned the room, he looked for something that might jog his memory. The old clock on the mantel, the painting of a Civil War soldier above the mantel and the old sword that hung above the picture meant nothing to him. He continued to look around the room. None of the furnishings or the other pictures on the walls looked familiar to him. He did not realize that these things should mean nothing to him as he had never been here before.

He turned his head and looked over at Becky. Who was the woman who seemed so concerned about him? She was a beautiful woman, whoever she was; but what was she to him? What part did she play in his life?

Matt's thoughts were disturbed when Sam walked into the living room. Who was the gray-haired man who had helped him? He understood he was Becky's father, but what was Sam to him?

"Did you rest well?" Sam asked quietly.

"Yes."

"Are you hungry?"

"Yes, I guess I am."

"I'll fix us some lunch in just a minute."

"Ah, Mr. McCullen?"

"Please, call me, Sam."

"Sam, are we related somehow?"

"No, I don't believe we are. Yesterday was the first time I ever laid eyes on you."

"Oh," he replied disappointedly.

Matt was as confused as ever. If he was not related to these people; and he did not belong here in the house, then where did he belong? He seemed to understand how he got here, but where had he come from and where had he been going?

Sam walked over to Becky, reached out and put his hand on her shoulder. He did not want to disturb her, but if she slept much longer like she was, she would surely get a stiff neck.

"Honey, honey," Sam repeated as he gently shook Becky's shoulder.

It took a few seconds for it to register in her mind that someone was trying to wake her. She turned and looked up to see her father smiling down at her.

"What's wrong?" she asked as she turned and looked toward Matt. He was awake and was watching her. She rubbed the back of her neck as she tried to get the stiffness out.

"Nothing's wrong. I thought you would like to have some lunch. Our guest said he's hungry."

"Oh, okay."

"What would you like for lunch? Soup and sandwiches be okay?" Sam asked their guest.

"That would be fine."

"What kind of soup do you like?"

Almost as soon as Sam asked the question, he realized that Matt might not be able to answer him. He wished that he had not asked the question at all, but just gave him some soup and hoped he liked it.

Matt looked at Sam as if his question had been the most difficult question he had ever been asked. He could not think of any kind of soup, let alone his favorite. He did not know if he even liked soup.

"Tell you what, I'll fix some vegetable soup. If you don't like it, we'll try something else," Becky suggested.

"Sounds like a good idea to me," Sam replied with a note of relief in his voice.

Becky stood up and went out into the kitchen. While she prepared the soup, Sam sat down next to Matt. Sam was trying to figure out the best way to help the young man.

"Do you remember anything, anything at all?" Sam asked as he looked into Matt's eyes.

"No," he replied after giving it some thought.

Sam noticed a hint of frustration in his voice. It had to be hard not to be able to remember anything about your past, he thought.

"Well, I wouldn't worry too much about it. It may take awhile, but once you get back to familiar surroundings your memory will come back."

"Where are these familiar surroundings?"

"That I don't know. Once we can get you into town, we can check with the police. They might be able to help find out who you are."

"How long will that be?"

"Two or three, maybe four days."

"Would it be all right if I look around your place while I'm here?" Matt asked.

"Sure, as soon as you're strong enough. What do you think you might find?"

"I don't know. Maybe, I will find something that will help me remember."

"You're certainly welcome to make yourself at home for as long as you like."

Sam could see no harm in letting him wander around the farm. There was always the chance that he would see something that might jog his memory.

"Thank you," Matt replied. He had no idea what he might find, but it was the only hope he had at the moment.

Becky interrupted Matt's thoughts when she came into the living room. He watched her as she walked across the room toward him.

"Would you like to eat in here, or do you feel up to coming to the kitchen?" she asked him.

"I would like to eat in the kitchen if you don't mind."

"Okay, but give me a minute."

Becky reached down and took the blanket from around his legs and put it on the sofa. She then leaned down and helped him to his feet.

He was feeling a little light-headed and put his arm around her for support. As he leaned against her, he could smell the soft delicate fragrance of her hair. He tried to remember if he had smelled that same fragrance before, but could not remember it.

As soon as his head cleared a little, Becky began to guide him toward the kitchen. She had her arm wrapped around him and he had his arm over her shoulder. After just a few steps, he seemed to be able to regain his balance by himself and did not need as much support. She sensed that it would not be long before he would be able to get around without her help.

Once in the kitchen, Sam pulled out a chair for Matt while Becky helped him into it. Matt watched as Becky turned toward the stove, filled each bowl with soup and set them on the table.

The smell of the soup did not bring back any memories for Matt, either. He tasted the soup. It was very good, but he could not remember ever having eaten anything like it before.

The three of them sat in silence and ate their lunch. Each one of them was deep in their own thoughts. It would be awhile before anyone, even Matt, would be able to understand what he was experiencing.

CHAPTER FIVE

Matt enjoyed the vegetable soup and the grilled cheese sandwich very much. He could not remember if he had ever had a lunch like the one he was enjoying before, but it did not really matter. The food was good, and his energy level seemed to improve with every bite. He was beginning to feel much better.

After lunch, Sam excused himself from the table and went outside. Becky got up and began clearing away the dirty dishes. Matt stayed at the table and soon found himself watching Becky's every move.

As she stretched to reach up to one of the higher cupboards, her sweatshirt pulled up above her waist. The jeans she wore caressed the smooth flowing lines from her narrow waist, down over her hips and on down her legs.

She turned around in time to catch him watching her. It did not bother her that he was looking at her. After all, she found him to be very handsome and she liked to look at him, too. She smiled, moved toward to the table and sat down across the table from him.

"Feeling better?" Becky asked.

"Yes, much better."

"How's your headache?"

"It's almost gone. I think the good meal helped a lot, and it was good."

"Would you like a cup of coffee?"

"Yes, that would be nice."

Becky got up and poured him a cup of coffee. However, she did not sit back down with him. Instead, she finished cleaning up the kitchen.

"I have to go take care of the horses. Would you like me to help you back to the living room?"

"Would it be all right if I just sit here for a little while?"

"Sure, but I'll be gone for the better part of an hour. Are you sure you will be okay?"

"I'll be fine. I would like to just sit here if you don't mind."

"Okay," Becky said as she turned and started for the back door.

Matt watched her as she walked out onto the porch. He noticed that she looked back to see if he was still sitting at the table before she disappeared around the corner and out of sight.

Sipping at his coffee, he gazed off into the other room. He was not looking at anything special. He was staring off into space and thinking.

Suddenly, there was another flash that went through his mind. It was as if a picture of someone had been flashed in front of him, but it lasted a split second longer than the first time. What little his mind allowed him to see told him that it was a woman. It was so quick that he could not make out the woman's features very well, but his mind had let him see that the woman had short blond hair and blue eyes.

From what little registered, he thought she was about his age or a maybe little younger, he could not be sure. He did not know who the woman was or why his mind would let him see her, but he guessed that she must have some importance in his life.

The sudden flash of someone, who was a complete stranger to him, disturbed him. He seemed to understand that his mind was trying to piece together the many fragments of his past. Yet, it made him wonder if he would ever really remember his past, and if he did, would it be a past that he would want to remember.

Matt tried to think of the woman in the hope that she would appear in his mind's eye again. If he could get a better look at her, he might remember who she was, and what part she played in his life. No matter how hard he tried, he was unable to visualize her again.

Giving up, he at least felt he was making some progress, however small it might be. He had seen the same vision twice in just a matter of hours. It gave him hope that his memory was trying to come back.

He looked around the kitchen, but found nothing that he felt was familiar. Carefully placing his hands on the edge of the table, he pushed himself up. Once on his feet, he stood for a minute to make sure he could stand without help. Being very careful, he slowly worked his way to the back door using the table, backs of chairs and the counter for support.

Once he got to the back door, he leaned against the doorframe and looked out toward the ridge. Somewhere up on that ridge his life, as he had once known it, had come to an abrupt end. He wondered if his life would ever be the same, or if he would want it to be the same.

As he looked at the thickly wooded hillside, he knew that he would have to regain a lot of his strength before he would be able to climb up there. The thought occurred to him that if he could find the airplane he was supposed to have flown, he might also be able to find some of his past. It was a long shot for sure, but what else could he do.

Matt's thoughts were interrupted when Sam suddenly came around the corner of the house. He watched Sam as he came toward the porch.

"Well, you look better. How are you feeling?" Sam asked.

"Pretty good. I'm a little weak, but I feel better."

"It's good, that you feel better. Are you coming out or going back in?"

"I was just trying to decide that very thing."

"Okay, but might I suggest you don't overdo it. If you feel tired, or your head begins to hurt, you better stop and rest."

"I will. Where's Becky?"

"She's out in the barn taking care of the horses. That might be a little far for you, just yet. If you want to see her horse, you can see him in the paddock from the front porch."

"Thank you."

Matt turned around slowly and went back inside the house. Taking his time, Matt walked through the house to the living room. As he walked across the living room, he could see Becky through the front door. She was at the fence of the paddock stroking the head of a large black horse. The horse seemed to respond to her and seemed to enjoy having her touch its nose.

Matt's attention was disturbed by the sound of a horse coming from down the lane. He saw Becky turn and look toward the sound. The way she smiled, it must be someone she knew and probably knew well. Matt moved over next to the door just in time to see a tall man wearing a slicker and a wide brimmed hat riding up toward the paddock on a large chestnut colored horse.

The man rode up to the fence and dismounted in one smooth flowing motion. He tied his horse to the fence and took off his hat as he walked up in front of Becky. He then reached out to her.

Matt watched as the newcomer put his hands on her shoulders and gently pulled her to him. Becky put her hands flat against his chest as if to prevent him from coming too close. He leaned down to kiss her, but she turned her head to one side just enough that in order for him to kiss her, he had to kiss her on the cheek. She did not seem to be resisting him very much, yet it was clear that she did not want him to kiss her on the lips, either.

Matt could not understand the feelings that came from deep inside him. For some unknown reason, he did not like the idea of the stranger holding Becky and trying to kiss her. What possible difference should it make to him? She was not his wife or even his girlfriend. He did not even know her, or so he had been told. She had helped him and that appeared to be the total sum of their relationship.

Becky turned away from Billy Joe and started toward the house. He quickly moved up alongside her with his hat still in his hand. He put his arm around behind her and walked with her as she walked toward the house.

Matt stepped through the door and out onto the porch. He noticed that the stranger appeared to be rather handsome, with broad shoulders, strong chin and long dark wavy hair. He wondered who the man was.

Becky glanced up toward the porch and saw Matt leaning against the door before Billy Joe saw him. A broad smile came over her face, as she looked up at the pilot, obviously pleased to see that he was able to get around fairly well by himself.

However, Billy Joe stopped suddenly in his tracks when he finally saw Matt leaning against the door, while Becky continued on toward the house. It was clear that Billy Joe was surprised to see another man at the house. Billy Joe gave Matt the once-over. It was easy to see from the look in Billy Joe's eyes that he had taken an instant dislike to Matt.

It was also clear to Matt that Billy Joe was not at all pleased to find someone else here. Matt wondered what business it was of Billy Joe's who was here. It was not his farm.

"It's good to see you up and around," Becky said as she started toward the steps of the porch.

"What do you mean by 'up and around'?" Billy Joe asked as he quickly stepped up to Becky, then reached out and grabbed her by the arm.

Billy Joe was a very jealous man when it came to Becky. In his mind, she was his, and that was all there was to it. His temper flared when he realized that a total stranger had been staying in the McCullen's house, and for how long he did not know.

Becky turned and looked up at Billy Joe. Her surprised look quickly turned to anger when she saw his temper was flaring up over something that was none of his business. By the sudden fire in Becky's eyes, and the stern look on her face, it was easy to see that she did not like the implication Billy Joe had made with his question, nor did she like the way he had grabbed her arm and held her.

"Just who the hell do you think you are?" she said as she jerked her arm free of his grip.

Matt started to step forward, but hesitated. He would like to punch the jerk in the nose, but he also knew that he did not have the strength to take on anyone, not yet.

"Let's get one thing very straight, right here, right now. You don't own me, Billy Joe. No one does. You don't tell me what to do, or anything else for that matter."

"What's happened to you?" he said surprised at the reprimand he was getting.

Billy Joe looked at her as if she had gone over the edge. He had never had any woman talk to him like that before, including Becky. He was not sure how to respond to it. He certainly didn't like it.

"Nothing has happened to me."

"Nothing! You bring a complete stranger into your house and you say 'nothing' is wrong with you."

"You don't tell me what to do. Don't you ever forget that. I think you had better leave."

Billy Joe turned and looked up at Matt leaning against one of the pillars on the porch. It was easy to see the hate in Billy Joe's eyes. Billy Joe looked back at Becky, turned on his heels and stomped off across the lane toward his horse.

Pulling his hat down on his head, he grabbed the reins of his horse and jerked them loose from the fence. Swinging up into the saddle, he pulled the reins around hard as he turned the horse and kicked him in the sides. The horse lunged forward and took off at a full run down the lane.

Matt looked over at Becky just as Billy Joe and his horse disappeared around a bend in the lane and behind some trees. He watched Becky as she continued to look down the lane. He did not like the look on her face. She looked as if she had just lost a good friend. Matt wondered what Billy Joe meant to her. Was he just a good friend of hers, possibly her boyfriend, or possibly something more?

Slowly, Becky turned back toward the porch. She looked up at Matt. A soft smile replaced the concerned look.

"I'm sorry. Billy Joe is a very jealous man. He doesn't like me to be around other men."

"I'm the one who should be sorry. I didn't mean to be the cause of a disagreement between you and your boyfriend."

Becky offered no comment. She did not really consider Billy Joe her boyfriend since they had gotten out of high school, and she had gone to the city. She did date him every once in awhile when she was home, but that was about it. She thought that she should say something to Matt about her relationship with Billy Joe, but decided to simply drop the subject.

Matt started to turn around and go back into the house. Becky quickly moved up beside him and slipped her arm around him for support. He looked down at her as she tried to help him. He almost told her that he did not need her help, but the feel of her arm around him was too nice to simply dismiss. He liked having her hold him even if he did not need it.

Putting his arm behind her neck and over her shoulder, he let her help him back into the house. She led him back to the easy chair. He sat down in the chair and watched her as she walked across the room and sat down on the sofa.

CHAPTER SIX

Matt spent the better part of the evening sitting in a chair watching the glow of the fire as he tried to recall his past. The crackling of the wood as it slowly burned kept his attention for a long time, but he was unable to remember his past. He could hear the sounds of the crickets and the occasional sound of a bug as it flew into the screen in an effort to get inside the house to the flame of the oil lamp setting on the table.

His gaze moved slowly around the room, examining it in detail. Sam was across the room in his big overstuffed chair. He had fallen asleep shortly after dinner and looked so much at peace that Matt wondered if it was the kind of lifestyle he had once enjoyed, or had he lived in an entirely different world.

Suddenly, there seemed to be an explosion of bright lights in his head, but it quickly subsided. Then there appeared to be a log, or a large tree branch rushing toward his face. He tried to duck, but it was too late. Yet, he did not feel anything as it seemed to hit him.

Realizing that it was his mind playing tricks on him and giving him brief glimpses of his past, he leaned back in the chair and closed his eyes.

The realism of the vision caused his heart to pound rapidly and his breathing came in short, hard breaths while little beads of sweat appeared on his forehead. What he had seen had been only in his mind, yet it had appeared to him to be as real as if it had actually happened at that very moment.

"Are you all right?" Becky asked noticing that he was breathing hard.

Matt opened his eyes and turned to look at her. He could see the deep concern in her eyes and wanted to explain what was happening to him, but he could not explain what he did not understand himself.

"I'm fine," he said as he tried to regain his composure.

Becky could see the sweat on his forehead. It caused her to worry. She was convinced that he must have had another vision. What was it he saw? Whatever it was, she was convinced that it had frightened him a great deal. She also began to understand that it was going to be a difficult time for him. He would need all the support she could give him.

"Can I get you anything?" she asked.

"No. No, thank you. You have done more than enough already."

Matt turned his face away and leaned back in the chair. He closed his eyes in the hope that sleep would come and give him rest. Sleep would continue to elude him for some time. It finally came, but only after he was able to get his mind to relax.

Becky returned to her book, but it was almost impossible for her to concentrate on it. It had been a very hard day for both of them, and she felt inadequate when it came to helping him. She found herself attracted to the man who now appeared to be sleeping not more than ten feet from her.

Becky's thoughts turned from Matt to Billy Joe. She knew that she had hurt Billy Joe's feelings and upset him by having a stranger in the house, but he did not have the right to say anything about it. Billy Joe had made no effort to find out why Matt was here, or to trust Becky's judgment.

It did not matter to Billy Joe that Matt had been in an airplane crash, and that she was just trying to help him. It also did not seem to matter to him that it was Sam's house, and not Becky's.

She began considering her relationship with Billy Joe and realized that it had been slowly deteriorating since she left to work in the city. Although she had been losing interest in him for some time, she still felt sort of a fondness for him. It bothered her that Billy Joe had treated her judgment with so little thought for her feelings.

It upset her that Billy Joe was such a jealous person. She remembered how angry he had gotten with her when she told him that she was moving to the city to find a job and go to school. He had even tried to stop her from leaving, but she left anyway.

She had found a job in the city and did go to school at a local university where she received her degree in Business Administration. If Billy Joe had his way, she would have married him right out of high school and they would have lived together on his father's farm raising lots of kids.

Becky liked Billy Joe's folks very much, but she did not love Billy Joe enough to marry him and raise a family with him. It was not that she did not want a family. She just did not want to raise a family with Billy Joe. There was a big wide wonderful world out there, and she wanted to see some of it before she settled down. Becky and Billy Joe had simply grown apart over the years. She understood that, but Billy Joe was still trying to hang onto the past.

Becky's thoughts were suddenly disturbed by an outcry from Matt. She looked at him and noticed that he seemed to still be sleeping. It was as if he were having a terrible nightmare. She put her book on the end table and quickly went to his side. She knelt down beside the chair and took his hand in hers. She held his hand while gently rubbing the back of it.

Matt did not wake up, but he seemed to calm down as soon as she touched him. Within seconds, he was once again in a quiet, restful sleep. She thought about moving back to her chair, but was afraid that he would not sleep as well if she did. Instead, she curled up against the side of the chair and laid her head down on his leg. Closing her eyes, she quickly fell asleep.

* * * *

Matt woke to the sound of a rooster crowing somewhere outside. As he opened his eyes, he looked down and saw Becky leaning against the chair with her head resting on his leg. He did not remember that she had been sitting there when he fell asleep, but he was sure that she had spent almost the entire night at his side.

He wanted to reach out and touch her, but decided not to wake her, not just yet. Instead, he took the opportunity to look at her. Her shoulder length dark brown hair looked soft and shiny as it cascaded over her shoulders. Her complexion was as smooth and creamy as pure silk. Although she appeared to be as peaceful and delicate as a small butterfly, he knew from yesterday that her look could have the sting of a hornet, and her tongue could be as sharp as a cat's claw.

Matt could not resist touching her any longer. He reached out and lightly touched her hair. It was as soft and silky as it looked. He felt her move slightly as he lightly ran his fingers over her hair.

"Good morning," he said softly.

She did not move, but let him continue to run his fingers over her hair.

"Good morning," she whispered.

Nothing more was said as they enjoyed the closeness they felt for each other at that moment. She still held his hand in hers and she squeezed it slightly.

Suddenly, he took his hand off her hair and pulled his other hand away from hers. Becky sat back on her heels and turned to look up at him. Why did he pull away from her, she wondered? What had she done?

"I'm sorry. I shouldn't be here with you like this," he said nervously.

"Why not?" Becky asked, surprised at his reaction.

He turned and looked away from her.

"It just isn't right. Not until I find out who I am."

Becky did not understand the sudden change. They had done nothing wrong. She could see nothing wrong with them being together, enjoying each other's company for a few minutes. Was it something he saw in his dream last night? Was there something that he did not want to tell her? He was pushing her away for no reason, at least no reason that made any sense to her.

Becky straightened her shoulders, stood up and looked down at him. Matt wanted her to stay, but he could see that he had hurt her feelings and did not know how to make it right.

"I'll go fix breakfast," she said flatly.

Matt watched her as she turned and walked briskly toward the kitchen. He hated himself for hurting her, but he just could not let himself get involved with anyone right now. He had to find out who he was before he could let himself get involved with her. The thought crossed his mind that he may not like what he found out about himself, but that was all the more reason for him not to get involved with her. He could end up hurting her.

"How we doing this morning?"

Matt's thoughts were abruptly interrupted by the question. He looked up to see Sam standing in the doorway looking at him.

"Not as well as I had hoped," Matt replied.

"What do you mean by that?"

Sam was worried by his response. He did not like the look on Matt's face, either. He was not sure if Matt was in pain, or if something else was troubling him.

"Nothing, really," Matt said trying to avoid an explanation.

"Breakfast will be ready soon," Sam said not wanting to be too nosy.

Sam turned and went out to the kitchen. He did not like the answer he got, but if Matt did not want to talk about it, that was his business.

Within a few minutes, Matt joined Becky and Sam in the kitchen. There was very little conversation while they ate. It may have had something to do with the chill in the air, and not from the weather. After they had finished, Matt watched Becky clear the table while her father went outside.

"I'm sorry," he said when she had her back to him.

She stopped what she was doing, turned around and looked at him. She could see in his eyes that his apology was sincere and that he had not meant to hurt her feelings.

"It's all right," she replied with a sigh. "I'm sure that you have a lot of things on your mind."

"That's just it. I don't have anything on my mind. I mean I can't remember anything. I don't even know who I am," he said with a strong note of frustration.

Becky stepped up to the table, pulled out a chair and sat down across the table from him. She reached across the table to him and put her hand over his. She wanted to tell him that everything was going to be all right, but she really did not know if it would be or not. She looked into his eyes as she tried to figure out what to say to him that would make him feel better.

"I haven't the faintest idea what you are going through," she began softly. "I have no way of understanding, but I do know that I will be here for you, and I will help you in any way I can. All you have to do is let me help you, even if it's just to hold your hand when you're hurting."

Becky's hand felt warm and soft against his. Her words were kind and gentle, and he wanted to believe her. He wanted to take her in his arms and hold her, but he could not do it. He squeezed her hand gently and she smiled at him. It seemed that a simple squeezing of her hand would be enough of an answer, at least for now.

He liked being with her, but if he did not change the subject he might find himself in her arms. That was just the thing that he needed to avoid, at least until he knew if he was free to care so much for her. Not knowing was the hardest part of all of it.

Gently pulling his hand out from under hers, he looked at her and said, "One thing I would like to do is take a shower."

"That will be easy," she smiled, almost glad that he decided to talk about something else. "But the water will not be very warm. The power has been out for a couple of days."

"A cool shower might feel good."

"Okay. Come on," she said as she stood up. "I'll show you where the shower is. I'll find you some clean clothes."

Matt stood up and followed her up the stairs to her bedroom. He stopped at the door and looked in as if he was afraid to enter her room. It was a beautiful room with lacy curtains of pale blues and pinks. The spread on the large old four poster bed was of the same colors. The room looked delicate, like her.

"This is a beautiful room," he commented as he looked across the room at her.

"Thank you. My mother decorated it for me when I was in high school."

Matt noted a touch of sadness in her voice. He guessed that her mother was no longer alive.

"The bathroom's in here," she said as she pointed to a door.

Matt crossed the room to the door and looked in. The bathroom was done in the same colors as the bedroom.

"My mother died of cancer just before I graduated from high school." For some reason, she felt that she should tell him.

"I'm sorry," he replied as he turned to look at her.

She smiled at him.

"The towels are on the rack and there is soap in the soap dish. I'll get you some clean clothes and lay them out on my bed."

Matt watched her as she turned and left the room. He closed the bathroom door and undressed. Turning on the water, he stepped into the shower. The water was cold and it took him a minute or two to adjust to it. Once he was used to the cold water, it felt good running over his skin. It seemed to refresh him.

He quickly lathered up and rinsed off. The water was a little too cold, however, to spend very much time in it. He shut off the water and took a big towel off the rack. The soft towel felt good against his skin. He jerked suddenly when he tried to briskly rub his head with the towel. The bump on his head was still very tender and shot a sharp pain through him.

Looking in the mirror, the black and blue marks on his head, shoulders and chest were clear signs that something violent had happened to him. While looking into the mirror, a vision quickly passed through his mind. It was the same one he had seen last night, only the vision lasted longer and did not frighten him as much. The marks on his body told him that what he was seeing in his mind was what had happened to him.

For the first time, he was truly convinced that what Becky had told him was the truth. He had crashed an airplane into the mountains. Although one of the many questions that ran through his mind had been answered, still more unanswered questions took its place. Questions like, was he the one flying the airplane, or was there someone else flying it. Where was he going, or where was he coming from? What was he doing in an airplane?

Matt finished drying off and wrapped the towel around his waist, then opened the door to Becky's bedroom. Looking into the room, he saw that she had laid out some clean clothes for him on the bed. It was a good thing that Sam was about the same size as he was, or he would have had little or nothing to wear.

Matt dressed, then sat on the edge of the bed to put on the tennis shoes that had been left for him. The shoes fit pretty well, even though they were about a half size too big. At least he would be able to get outside and walk around a little, maybe begin to get a little exercise.

He stood up and walked over to the window. Becky's room looked out over the paddocks where her big black horse was grazing. It was such a peaceful picture from her bedroom window that it was easy for him to understand why she liked the room so much. From here, she would be able to see a long way down the meadow toward the creek.

Mark's attention was drawn toward some movement just off to the left side of the valley in the trees. He was not sure what it was, but it did not seem to belong there. Straining to see what was in the shadows of the forest near the edge of the meadows was not easy, but gradually it registered in his mind what he was seeing. It was the big chestnut colored horse that Billy Joe had been riding yesterday, but he could not see Billy Joe anywhere.

The horse appeared to be tied to a tree. If that was the case, then Billy Joe must be out in the barn, or somewhere near by. Maybe, behind the barn. What possible reason could Billy Joe have for sneaking around the barn, Matt wondered?

Matt did not like the idea of Billy Joe sneaking about, but on the other hand, it was really none of his business. If Billy Joe wanted to talk to Becky without anyone else around, that was his business. He turned around and sat back down on the bed to finish dressing.

CHAPTER SEVEN

As Matt put on the shoes he had been given, he kept thinking about Billy Joe being out there sneaking around behind the barn. He wondered if Becky had gone out to the barn while he was in the shower. If she had, did she know that Billy Joe was out there somewhere? The more he thought about it, and remembered Billy Joe's temper, the more it troubled him.

As soon as Matt was finished dressing, he went downstairs. Looking around, he found no one in the house. He stepped out onto the porch and looked toward the barn. There was no one in sight. He walked to the end of the porch and stopped suddenly when he saw Sam working in his garden next to the house.

"Well, it's good to see you up and about. Feel better after your shower?" Sam asked as he stopped hoeing and stretched.

"Ah, yes."

"Pretty cold, I'll bet," Sam said with a grin.

"Yes, it was," Matt replied as he glanced down toward the barn. "I was wondering if you know where Becky might be?"

"I believe she's in the barn. She's feeding the horses and checking on her mare."

Sam was a little concerned about the determined look on Matt's face, but he had always made it a point of not butting into other people's business. After Matt stepped off the porch and started for the barn, Sam watched him for a minute then returned to his work in the garden.

Matt had gone only about fifty feet from the porch when he stopped suddenly and covered his face with his hands as another vision passed through his mind. All he could see of the vision was rolling clouds; violent, dark, angry clouds that frightened him for a second. Again, the vision was so real to him that it was hard for him to believe that it was all in his mind. As soon as the vision passed, he just stood there looking toward the barn while he took some time to regain his composure and slow his breathing.

As soon as he was able, he continued across the yard. He noticed that the big doors at the end of the barn were open. Walking up to the doors, he stopped and listened, but heard nothing. Stepping inside the barn, he looked around, but there was no one in sight. Again he listened, only it was different, he heard voices. They seemed to be coming from up above him, up in the hayloft. Walking over to the ladder, he looked up as he reached out and took hold of the ladder. Just as he was about to put his foot on the first rung, he stopped. He thought about going up, but decided against it. Instead, he listened for some clue as to what was going on.

"I want you to leave."

Becky's voice seemed calm and clear. Her comment sounded more like a simple request than a demand. Matt could see no reason to interfere in their discussion. After all, he was a guest.

"What the hell's gotten into you? Ever since you went off to that damn school, I ain't good enough for you."

Matt turned away from the ladder and was about to leave, but the bitter tone of Billy Joe's voice caused him to stop. The sound of Billy Joe's voice was much different than that of Becky's. He did not want to interfere, but he did not want to leave Becky alone with Billy Joe when he sounded so angry. He had seen Billy Joe's temper flare up before. With that kind of temper, he had no idea what Billy Joe might be capable of doing.

"The school didn't have anything to do with it. We simply grew apart and went our separate ways. That's all there is to it," Becky said trying to remain calm in an effort to calm Billy Joe's anger.

"That's bull. You never thought I was good enough for you," he stated sharply.

"Billy Joe, we had a lot of fun together over the years. Why can't you understand that times change and people change, too?"

"You've certainly changed," he rebutted angrily.

"Yes, I have changed, but that doesn't mean we can't be friends."

Becky could see that no matter what she said nothing was going to change the way Billy Joe saw things. His anger had gotten in the way of reason.

"I don't want to be friends," he blurted out.

"Then I think you had better go. I don't think you should come back until you can come over as a friend," Becky said firmly, but without raising her voice.

"You can't just dump me for some dumb pilot that falls out of the sky. I'm going into town and see the sheriff. I'm going to find out who this guy is," Billy Joe said with a threatening tone in his voice.

"Why don't you just do that? And while you're at it, you can get off my father's land and stay off," Becky said, unable to control her anger any longer.

"You're not going to tell me what to do, and you're not going to dump me for some guy who doesn't even know who the hell he is," Billy Joe said as he reached out and grabbed her by the arms.

"Let go of me," Becky demanded angrily.

Matt heard the sudden change in Becky's voice. She sounded frightened. He turned back to the ladder and climbed up to the loft as fast as he could. It was a strenuous climb for him. By the time he reached the top of the ladder, he was breathing very hard.

"Let go of her," Matt demanded.

Billy Joe turned around to see Matt leaning against a post as he tried to catch his breath. Billy Joe almost laughed at the demands made by a man who could hardly climb a ladder without stopping to rest.

"Well, well. If it isn't the flyboy. You've finally come out of hiding."

Matt could hear the intense dislike in Billy Joe's voice, and he could see the hate in his eyes. He also noticed that Billy Joe had not let go of Becky's arm. He pushed himself up as straight as possible. It was easy to see that he would be no match for Billy Joe in his present condition, but he had to make a stand.

"I said, `let go of her!'"

Billy Joe let go of Becky's arm and stepped toward Matt. Matt had to step back slightly to give Billy Joe room to pass him, but gave no indication that he was going to back down.

"I don't know who you are, but you're going to wish you had never seen this place."

Matt made no attempt to argue with him and made every effort to show Billy Joe that he was not afraid of him. He had no idea what Billy Joe might do, but he did not trust him.

Billy Joe looked back at Becky. "This guy had better be gone when I get back from the sheriff's office."

"He can stay as long as he wants and there is nothing you can do about it," she countered.

"We'll see about that."

Matt stepped aside as Billy Joe moved toward the ladder. Billy Joe turned and started down the ladder. He stopped and looked at Becky, then at Matt.

"We'll meet again, you can count on it."

It was clear that his comment was meant as a threat and Matt planned to treat it as such. Matt was sure they would meet again, but just where and when were the only things that had been left unsaid.

As soon as Billy Joe was out of sight, Matt leaned back against one of the posts. Although he had been regaining his strength fast, it was still a little too soon after the crash to be getting very energetic.

"Are you all right?" Becky asked as she took hold of his arm.

"I guess I shouldn't try to the play hero until I'm a little stronger."

Becky smiled at him. It pleased her a great deal that he was willing to try to be her hero, even if he didn't have the strength to back it up.

"I don't know, I think you did rather well," she said with a smile.

"Yeah, but it's a good thing he didn't throw a punch at me. I would have folded up like an accordion."

Matt pushed himself away from the post and moved over to a bale of hay. He sat down on the bale and Becky sat down beside him. She took hold of his arm, which he did not mind at all. They looked into each other's eyes. Slowly, they leaned toward each other. Their lips met in a warm gentle kiss.

Becky liked the tenderness of his kiss and the warmth of his lips. His kiss sent a feeling through her that she had never felt before from such a light kiss. It made her want to simply melt into his arms.

A vision suddenly passed through Matt's mind causing him to pull back away from Becky. His sudden pulling away startled her. At first she was confused, but she quickly realized what was happening to him. It worried her a great deal, but she did not know what she could do to help him. She simply watched him and held his hand as she waited for it to pass.

It was clear to her that each time he had one of these brief visions, he was putting together little pieces of the puzzle that was his past life. The uncertainty of what his past life was like, and if someone he loved was waiting for him somewhere else, caused her concern. She knew that they should avoid any romantic relationship, at least until they found out if he might have a family somewhere.

Becky let go of his arm, stood up and looked away. She sudden realization that she might be romantically interested in him shook her deeply. Was she really falling for him, or was she just caring for him like she did for the many sick and injured animals she had taken care of in the past? What was she going to do if they fell in love with each other, and then found out that he had a wife and family somewhere? She could not risk it. She could not let herself get involved with him. She could not let him get involved with her, either.

Becky turned around and looked at him. He was looking at her. She wanted to say something to him that would help him understand what was going on in her mind, but she could not say anything. He had enough problems without adding to them, she thought.

Matt had a pretty good idea what Becky was thinking. He was wondering the same thing. It would not be fair to her for them to fall in love. There were too many unanswered questions about his past. Somehow, he knew that it was not the area of the country that he was from. He was sure that he lived many miles from here, but where he did not know.

Matt watched as Becky walked over to the ladder and climbed down out of the loft. He wanted to go after her and tell her that he understood, but what did he understand? He understood that she cared about him very much even though she did not know him. He did not even know himself. He knew he cared about her, but he did not know her, either. He slumped down and put his head in his hands, his elbows on his knees. Why did life have to be so complicated, he thought? He began to feel tired and weary.

Suddenly, another vision passed through his mind, but it stayed long enough for him to understand it. What he saw was a tall slim blond who was screaming at someone. The woman was very angry, but he could not figure out why. Who was she angry at? What was she angry about? It was almost as if she were yelling at him.

As her words seemed to drift into his consciousness, he could almost hear the woman's voice and realized that she was screaming at him, but why? What had he done to make the woman so upset with him?

"You're never home any more. You spend all your time with that secretary of yours. You don't love me, and you certainly don't care about me any more."

In his mind, he could hear her just as if she were speaking to him at that very minute. Who is she? There was no answer to his question. Based on what she said, she must be someone that he cared about very much at one time. Is she an old girl friend, maybe his wife or possibly his ex-wife?

It was a major part of his past and a good size piece of the puzzle, but it still was not enough for him to be able to put it all together. Any answers he came up with now would still be just guesses. He did not have enough information to piece his past together.

* * * *

Once Becky reached the bottom of the ladder, she stopped to look back up toward the loft. It was clear that no matter how much she had not wanted to fall in love with the stranger, she could not help herself. She wanted to go back up the ladder and tell him that his past did not matter, but she could not do it. The truth was, it did matter. It mattered very much. Maybe it did not matter to her, but it mattered to him and that was enough.

As her eyes began to fill with tears, she turned and ran out of the barn. She ran out behind the barn and on into the woods. Once inside the woods, she ran up to a big oak tree, stopped and leaned against it. She began to cry openly.

As a small girl, the large oak tree had been her friend. It was the place where she would go when she could not turn to anyone else for comfort. It was her secret place. A place where she could have the privacy she needed to resolve her innermost conflicts. It was a place where she could come to think. Right now, she needed to cry. She could try to think after she let her emotions escape.

Gradually, her tears subsided and she began to regain control of herself. Sitting down at the base of the tree, she leaned back against it and tipped her head back. She knew deep down in her heart that she had no business falling in love with a man she knew nothing about, a man who could not even tell her his name or anything about his past. It was difficult enough that she had to watch him struggle to regain his strength, but she had to watch him as he tried to piece together his past. A past that she might later wish he never remembered.

Her mind wandered back to his kiss, a kiss that had touched her deeply. But why? Why had it touched her so deeply? It certainly was not the first time that she had been kissed by a man. She thought she was acting like a schoolgirl with her heart all aflutter, but she knew all too well that she was not a schoolgirl.

Her mind was full of questions, only not about Matt, but about herself. Why was she so taken by him? What was it about him that was different from other men she had known?

Pulling her legs up and wrapping her arms around them, she laid her chin down on her knees and looked out over the meadow.

Common sense told her to get hold of herself and act responsibly. It would be best in the long run if she knew more about him. She knew in her heart that it would not be wise to pursue any kind of relationship with him, at least until she knew more about him.

Becky spent the next few minutes thinking about how she had let her emotions govern her. It was not often that she did not keep herself under tight control. It was not like her to let anyone get to her like he did, but that was over. She firmly resolved that she would keep her emotions in check, at least until she knew him a lot better.

With her new resolution strongly framed in her mind, she was ready to face him again. She stood up straight and brushed the loose grass off her jeans. Now firm in her commitment, she started back toward the house.

CHAPTER EIGHT

Sam was still busy pulling weeds and hoeing in the garden when Becky returned to the house. He observed the way she carried herself, her back straight with her shoulders back and a strong look of determination on her face. Even as a small girl she had tried to hide her feelings in the same way. Having seeing her acting that way times before, it caused Sam to wonder what might have happened in the barn.

Sam had also seen Matt come out of the barn. He had walked off down the lane toward the road with his head down and his hands jammed down in his pockets as if he were deep in thought. The actions of these two gave Sam reason to pause, but they were adults and it was none of his business. However, he could not let his only daughter worry so without at least making an attempt at trying to help her.

"What's the matter, honey?" Sam asked as he leaned against the hoe and looked up at her.

Becky stopped and turned toward her father. She wanted to talk to him about Matt, but she did not know what to say.

"Nothing," she said quietly.

"Hey now, this is your father you're talking to. I know you better than anyone, and I know when there is something troubling you. What is it?"

"Oh, daddy," she said with a long sigh.

"Come on, you can talk to me."

Sam leaned the hoe against the porch railing, walked over to the porch and sat down on the step. He motioned for Becky to sit down beside him. He took hold of her hand as she reluctantly sat down with him.

"What's the matter, Kitten?"

"I'm confused. In a way, I wish we could find out who he is, yet in another way I'm not sure I want to know."

"Are you afraid of what you might find out about him?"

Becky thought for a minute. "I guess maybe I am."

"Kitten, it's only normal to feel that way about someone you care about. Tell me, what happened?"

Becky looked at her father. She remembered how he had always helped her when she was confused. Even as a little girl he could tell when she needed someone to talk with and he was always there for her.

"Billy Joe was out in the barn," she stated flatly as she looked out across the lane toward the barn while she tried to put her thoughts together.

"I didn't see him come here."

"He came up from down by the creek on his horse."

"What's he doing sneaking around?"

"He's so jealous, Daddy," she said as she turned and looked back at her father. "He doesn't like, ah, our guest being here. Billy Joe got really upset and told me he was going to see the sheriff."

"Well, that's not all that bad an idea, is it?"

"No," she replied with a sigh.

"It probably would be a good idea to find out who this guy is, don't you think?"

"I guess so, but Billy Joe has no right to interfere."

"I'll agree with that, but Billy Joe has known you for a long time. Don't you think that he might be trying to protect you?"

"I don't need his protection," she said defensively.

"Maybe not, but he does care about you a great deal."

Becky understood what her father was trying to tell her. Billy Joe had always looked out for her, all the way through school. She knew that he loved her, or at least he thought that what he felt for her was love.

"If he cares about me so much, why did he grabbed me by the arm and threatened our guest when he tried to make Billy Joe let go of me?"

Sam looked at his daughter with the deep concern of a loving father. It did not set well with him that his daughter was grabbed when she didn't want to be. As far as Sam was concerned, Billy Joe had gone too far. He would not tolerate anyone manhandling his daughter.

"Did he hurt you?"

"No, not really, but he threatened our guest and told him that they would meet again."

"Billy Joe has overstepped his bounds."

"I told him not to come back."

Sam nodded his approval of her decision to tell Billy Joe not to return, but he still wondered about her feelings for their guest.

"I saw our guest walking down the lane toward the road. Is there something wrong?"

"No, not really. He's worried that he may not like what he finds out about himself."

"Is that all he is worried about?"

"No, I don't think so," she replied not wanting to make more of it than necessary.

"Well, I can understand that. But a person can always change. I think that you have to give him some time. It's hard enough not to be able to remember your past, but it has got to be extremely difficult not to be able to remember what you're like, what you don't like, and what kind of a person you were. Not to know whether you're married or not. It's hard not to be able to remember the basic things about yourself. He needs time."

Becky looked into her father's eyes. It was clear that he understood, or at least had a good idea of what was going on between them. She thought about what he had said, and as usual her father was right. There was no way for her to know what Matt was going through. She should be trying to help him instead of putting more pressure on him. As she looked toward the lane, she realized how selfish she had been. She needed to find him and set things straight.

"Where did you say he was going?" she asked.

Becky had a new spark of life in her voice. She had been thinking of herself when she should have been trying to help Matt find his past. It was time to think about Matt, and help him.

"I saw him going down the lane toward the road," Sam replied.

Becky stood up and started off down the lane. She could not see Matt anywhere and was beginning to worry about him. If he just walked off, she was afraid that he could get lost. When she reached the road, she looked both ways, but did not see him. She did not know which way to turn.

Immediately, she blamed herself for him leaving. If anything else happened to him because of her selfishness, she would not be able to forgive herself.

Trying to decide which way to go, she glanced down at the ground. There in the mud were Matt's footprints. She instantly realized that to find him, all she would have to do would be to follow his tracks.

Following his tracks, she ran along the side of the road. She stopped suddenly when she saw him leaning against a tree. He had his back to her and his hands over his eyes. She walked up behind him, reached out and put her hand gently on his shoulder.

Matt was startled by her touch and swung around quickly. Becky jumped back and stared at him. She knew by the look in his eyes that he had another vision.

"Are you all right?" she asked softly.

He was breathing hard and sweat had beaded up on his forehead. Matt did not answer, but simply stared at her. He wanted to put his arms around her and hang onto her, but he could not move.

"Maybe, you should come back to the house with me," Becky said as she reached out a hand to him.

"I don't belong here," Matt said as if he had just realized his statement to be true.

Becky was frightened by his revelation. She wondered if he had seen his past and knew where he was from. The realization that he might want to leave pulled at her heart. She was not ready for him to leave. Besides, he was not well enough to go anywhere very far.

"I know you are not from here, but at least until you are better you should stay here," she said softly. "You can't go anywhere now. The roads are still washed out."

He looked from her face to the hand she still held out to him. His mind was filled with confusion and he felt disoriented. He had very little choice. He needed someone to help him.

Slowly, he reached out and took hold of her hand. The warmth and the softness of her small hand seemed to reassure him that it was all right to go with her. He was just discovering that he had strong feelings for her, but he was not sure that he should have those kinds of feelings. He was confused.

As they walked back toward the house, Matt looked at the woman walking beside him. She was looking straight ahead. He thought he could see a small tear in the corner of her eye, and was sure that he had hurt her somehow.

"I'm sorry," he said quietly.

"What are you sorry for?" Becky asked as she turned and looked at him.

"I'm sorry that I have hurt you. I didn't intend to disrupt your life and cause problems between you and your boyfriend."

"You didn't cause any problems between Billy Joe and me. He still thinks he is in love with me, and maybe he is. He just won't accept the fact that it's over between us and that it has been for a very long time."

As they approached the house, they saw that Sam had returned to working in the garden. They went inside and Matt sat down at the kitchen table while Becky set lunch on the table.

* * * *

Matt spent the next few days doing whatever he could to help around the farm. He cleaned stalls, fed and watered the animals and brushed the horses. Gradually, day by day, he regained his strength and endurance. The more he did, the more he began to like working around the farm. He seemed to get a lot of satisfaction out of the work he did, and he felt useful.

As each day went by, he also continued to have flashes of his past. Bit by bit, and piece by piece, he was beginning to put his past back together again. He did not share each little piece of his past with Becky. There were two other women in his past, but he was not sure of his relationship to them. He did not know if perhaps one of them might be his wife, or if they were simply old girlfriends. Until he knew what they meant to him, he would not tell Becky about them.

He tried to keep his distance from Becky by being polite, yet aloof, and by keeping himself busy. Until he knew who he was and what kind of a person he had been in the past, he felt it would be best to keep from getting too involved with her. He liked her very much, but without the knowledge of his past, he might hurt her. He did not want that to happen.

Matt was in the loft of the barn getting ready to throw down a bale of hay when he saw a sheriff's car drive up to the house. He stopped, set down the bale of hay and watched as the sheriff got out of the car and greeted Sam.

Matt could not hear what was being said, but it was clear that the sheriff was looking for him. It was also clear that Billy Joe had kept his word and told the sheriff that he was there. Matt did not want to cause Becky and her father any trouble, so he laid the bale hook on a bale of hay and climbed down out of the loft.

Becky was standing at the door of the barn looking toward the house. She had been watching the sheriff as well. When she heard Matt come up behind her, she turned and looked at him.

"The Sheriff is here," Becky said as she watched him for some kind of response.

"Yes, I know. I saw him drive up."

"What are you going to do?"

"I'm going to go talk to him."

"Are you sure that's a good idea. You could go out through the back of the barn into the woods until he leaves," she suggested.

Matt looked at her and wondered why she would make such a suggestion. Did she know something about him that he did not know, or was she just trying to give him more time to find out about himself?

"Why would I want to run away?"

"You are having those flashes of your past more often. It shouldn't be too much longer before you figure out who you are."

"I can't count on that. If the sheriff can find out who I am, maybe things will fall into place for me."

Becky could see the logic in his thinking, but the sooner he found out who he was, the sooner he would leave. Her head told her that he was right, but her heart told her to hang on to him for as long as possible.

"Will you walk up to the house with me?" he asked as he held out his hand.

Becky looked at his outstretched hand and took hold of it. After a brief hesitation, they began walking toward the house. It pleased her very much that he wanted her with him. She did not know what was going to happen, but the warmth of his hand seemed to give her the courage she needed.

As they approached the Sheriff, the Sheriff turned and looked at Matt. It was easy to see that he was carefully scrutinizing Matt. As he glanced at Becky, a smile came over his face.

"Hi, Becky. It's good to see you again. How is everything in the big city?"

"Just fine, I guess. I've been here for the past couple of weeks."

"Oh, I didn't know that."

Becky had known Sheriff Frank Stevens for many years. He and her father had been friends for as long as she could remember. She also knew him to be firm in his duties as the sheriff, but he was also a fair man. It gave her some relief to know that Sheriff Stevens was handling it personally.

"I guess you are the young man I've heard about?"

"Yes, sir," Matt replied.

"I understand that you do not know who you are, is that right?"

"Yes, sir."

"How about sitting down and talking with me for a couple of minutes?"

"Sure."

Matt walked with Sheriff Stevens, Sam and Becky up onto the porch. Becky sat down next to Matt on the porch swing while Sheriff Stevens sat down on a porch chair. Sam sat on the railing and leaned against one of the posts.

"Why don't you tell me what you do know about yourself?" Sheriff Stevens said politely.

"It isn't very much. I have had several flashes that seem to tell me a little about myself, but as of yet I haven't been able to put them together."

"Have you figured out what your name is, or possibly part of your name, maybe your initials?"

"No, sir. In one of my flashes I saw a name on a door. It seemed like it was the door to some kind of a business or office, but I'm not sure. These flashes come so quickly.

"I see," Sheriff Stevens said thoughtfully. "What was the name on the door?"

"I really don't remember. I do remember the letters "M" and "S" for some reason, but that is about it."

"I understand you're a pilot?"

"They tell me I am. They told me I crashed up on the ridge behind the house, but you will have to ask them about that."

"You must be a pilot. Sam tells me you were the only one in the plane when they got to it. Is it possible that there was someone else in the plane, someone who got out before Sam got there?"

"I'm sorry, Sheriff. I can't help you. I only know what they have told me about the plane. In one of my flashes I saw a branch coming through what looks like an airplane windshield and hitting me in the face, but that's about all. I don't remember if anyone else was in the plane."

"Maybe, you should come into town with me. I can put you up at the local hospital for evaluation while I run your fingerprints. If you've been in the service, or been arrested in the past, there would be a set of fingerprints on file somewhere."

"Can't he stay here with us?" Becky asked as she looked over at her father.

Sheriff Stevens looked at Becky, then at Sam. Becky's request seemed a little out of the ordinary to the sheriff, but after all he had already been here for several days.

"I don't see any reason why he can't stay here," Sam replied. "After all, he seems to be getting along pretty well, and his memory seems to be getting better, little by little. I don't see how it would help him any being moved to a less familiar place, or confining him to a hospital."

"What do you think?" Sheriff Stevens asked Matt. "You want to stay here?"

"If it's okay with you, I would just as soon stay here, at least for now. I've gotten kind of used to the place."

"Okay. I'll want to take your fingerprints and see if I can find out who you are. Do you have a problem with that?"

"I have no problem with that," Matt replied.

Matt waited on the porch while Sheriff Stevens got his fingerprint kit out of the car. After he fingerprinted Matt, the sheriff said goodbye to his friends and drove off down the lane.

Shortly after lunch, Matt returned to the barn to finish taking care of the horses. He did not talk very much as his mind was full of speculations on what Sheriff Stevens might find out about him. In some ways, he hoped that the sheriff would not find out anything. He was beginning to like it on the farm. He also liked Becky very much, much more than he probably should. He was even having serious thoughts about staying here after he found out who he was, if Sam and Becky would let him.

Matt worked hard around the barn in an effort to keep himself busy so that he did not have to think about anything, especially Becky. He had a couple of flashes while he worked, but they did not add much to what he had already pieced together. By dinnertime he was very tired and hungry. Shortly after dinner, he excused himself and went to bed.

Becky could understand why he was tired. He had worked very hard all afternoon. It seemed to her that he was working hard in an effort to avoid her, but she knew that he had a lot on his mind, a lot to think about.

Becky had a lot on her mind, too, and went to bed shortly after dinner. Sleep did not come easily for her. She was sure that when the sheriff figured out who Matt was, he would be leaving. She knew that their time together was limited.

She closed her eyes in an effort to get some sleep, but her mind kept reminding her of the warmth of the touch of his hand, and the emotions that his kiss had stirred in her. She had to ask herself if she was falling in love with him, but the answer was still not clear. Only after a great deal of tossing and turning did she finally drift off to sleep.

CHAPTER NINE

Becky woke to the birds singing outside her window, but she did not feel much rested. She had spent most of the night tossing and turning, trying to clear her mind so that sleep could come and give her rest. Looking over toward the window, she noticed that the sun was bright. The slight movement of the trees outside her window gave a hint of a gentle breeze. It seemed rather late, yet she was still tired. She glanced over at the clock on the bedside stand and discovered it was well past nine, much later than usual for her to be getting up.

Reluctantly, she climbed out of bed and went to the window. Looking out over the paddock, she saw their guest leaning against the fence petting her horse's forehead. It surprised her a little to see her horse enjoying the petting because he did not seem to make friends with strangers very easily. She smiled to herself as she watched them. It seemed to her to be the perfect picture, the way things should be.

Her feeling of contentment quickly dissolved as her thoughts turned to yesterday and Sheriff Stevens taking his fingerprints. It would be only a matter of time before the sheriff would return and be able to identify him. When that happened, he would walk out of her life and be gone forever.

There was no doubt in her mind that it would happen. It was inevitable. There had to be a way to stop it from happening, at least for a little while, she thought.

Suddenly, an idea came to her. If he was not here, not on the farm when the sheriff came back, then the sheriff would not be able to take him away from her. It was a beautiful day, a day that they could spend together. They could pack a lunch and ride to someplace where no one could find them.

Becky was not expecting any kind of a miracle. She knew it would only be for one day, but at least it would be a day that they could spend together without interruption from the rest of the world. As she looked out the window, she wondered if he would go along with her idea.

She turned away from the window and took off her nightie. Quickly, she dressed in jeans and a blouse. She put on some socks and slipped into her boots. After running a comb through her hair, she ran downstairs and through the living room.

Stepping out onto the front porch, she stopped and saw that he was still leaning against the fence. He seemed to be talking to the horse and the horse seemed to like him.

"He likes sugar cubes," Becky called out to him.

Matt turned to see Becky standing on the porch leaning against one of the post and smiling at him. She was a beautiful woman, he thought. Her long dark hair moved gently in the morning breeze. The colorful blouse she wore accented the lines of her firm breasts while her snug fitting jeans showed off the smooth flowing lines of her narrow waist and curved hips. It was impossible for him not to admire her as he walked toward the porch.

"It's about time you got up," he said as he smiled up at her.

"Have you had breakfast?"

"Yes, I had breakfast with your father."

"Where is he?"

"He went over to your neighbor's. I believe he said the Stanfords. It seems your neighbor needed some help with a plumbing problem, or something of that nature."

"Are the phones working?"

"No. Mr. Stanford came over on his horse."

"Jacob is always having plumbing problems," she replied with a smile.

"You look very nice this morning," Matt said as his eyes glanced over her again.

"Thank you," she replied shyly.

Having him look at her like he did made her feel very sexy. She liked feeling sexy for him.

She noticed that he seemed to be moving around more freely. His bruises must no longer be painful and the stiffness had apparently gone from his muscles, she thought. It pleased her very much to see that he was recovering so fast.

"Do you ride horses?"

Becky quickly realized that he probably did not remember if he rode horses or not. She hoped that he was not embarrassed because of her forgetfulness.

"I don't remember if I've ever ridden a horse before, but I'd be willing to try," he replied, wondering what she had in mind.

"I was thinking that we might go for a ride this morning," she suggested.

"I'd like that. Maybe, we could take a lunch, and you could show me around the valley?"

"Sure," Becky agreed, surprised by his suggestion of taking a lunch.

Becky could hardly contain her excitement. Matt apparently wanted to be with her as much as she wanted to be with him. She wondered if he had the same fears that she had, not knowing if they would ever have another chance to be together.

"I'm not real sure about saddling up a horse and things like that, so maybe it would be best if I make the lunch and you pick out the horses and saddle them."

Becky grinned and nodded her head in agreement. "I'll have the horses ready in about fifteen minutes."

"Good, it will take me at least that long to fix lunch."

Matt stepped up on the porch as Becky stepped passed him. He turned around and watched her as she walked toward the barn. She had a smooth and graceful gait, and a slight sway to her shapely hips. He smiled to himself, then turned around and went into the house.

Becky picked out a roan gelding for Matt that she knew was not only a good horse, but was fairly easy to ride and took commands well. As soon as the horse was saddled and ready to ride, she saddled a chestnut mare that she liked to ride. Both horses were large Morgans that had been raised by the McCullens from foals.

As soon as the horses were ready, she led them out of the barn and up to the porch. She tied them to the porch railing, took the saddlebags off the saddles and went in the house to see if she could help him prepare a lunch.

Walking into the kitchen, she saw that he had several packages wrapped in aluminum foil and a thermos bottle sitting on the table. He had his back to her and apparently had not heard her come in. When he turned around with a bottle of wine in his hand, he felt a little embarrassed. He hesitated for a second, then smiled.

"A little wine for our picnic lunch?" he asked sheepishly.

"Sure, but what are we having?"

"I have a couple of steaks, two ears of corn all ready buttered and salted, some sliced apples in cinnamon and butter, a thermos of coffee and a bottle of wine," he said as he pointed to each item on the table.

"I don't think we'll starve," she commented as she looked over the table.

"Is it too much?"

Matt was afraid that he might have gone a little overboard. It was really a dinner, but if they were going to be gone all day, he did not think that it would be all that much.

"No. It sounds great," she said with a smile.

"I thought that we might make a day of it, but if you would rather just have sandwiches or something like that, I can fix them."

"No, please. It sounds wonderful. I'll get a blanket to spread out on the ground."

Matt watched her turn around and disappear. He could hear Becky's footsteps as she went up the stairs for the blanket. He packed the food and utensils into the saddlebags along with the coffee and wine. Becky returned with a blanket rolled up and tucked under her arm.

"You ready?" she asked.

"I guess so," Matt replied as he picked up the saddlebags.

"I had better leave a note for Dad."

Matt stood by and watched her as she scribbled out a brief note to Sam telling him that they had decided to go for a ride and would be gone most of the day. When she finished, she leaned the note against the sugar bowl on he kitchen table. They walked out onto the porch together.

Matt stopped and looked at the two horses. He tried to remember if he had ever been riding before. As he thought about it, he decided that it really did not matter. Since he could not remember, it would be just the same as if he had never been on a horse before. He took in a deep breath and stepped off the porch.

"Which horse do I ride?"

"The roan, that one," Becky replied as she tied the blanket on the saddle of the horse that she was going to ride.

Matt handed one of the saddlebags to Becky. He moved around next to the roan, gently patted him on the neck, then swung his saddlebags over the back of the saddle. After securing the saddlebags, he untied the reins and stood next to the horse looking at the saddle and stirrups. He was unsure of himself so he waited and watched to see how Becky mounted her horse.

As soon as Becky was ready, she untied the reins, stepped around next to the horse, put her foot in the stirrup and swung gracefully into the saddle. She smiled as she watched Matt look over the horse, take a deep breath and carefully put his foot in the stirrup.

Her smile quickly faded when his foot slipped out of the stirrup and he leaned against the horse, resting his head against the saddle. She instantly knew that he was having another one of his visions. There was nothing she could do for him except wait until he regained control of himself. It always made her feel so helpless.

Matt hung onto the saddle horn as he tried to catch his breath. The vision had lasted for several seconds and revealed that he had been alone in the airplane when it crashed. Although it lasted only a few seconds, he could actually envision the airplane coming apart as it crashed.

Becky sat nervously waiting in the saddle until he let out a long sigh and straighten up. Maybe, it would be better if they stayed close to the house, she thought. She was about to suggest it to him when he raised his foot and put it back in the stirrup. With a lot less grace than Becky had shown, he pulled himself up onto the saddle. He turned and looked over at her and forced a smile.

"You ready?" he asked, still a little short of breath.

She could see the beads of sweat on his forehead, and he could see the worried look in her eyes. It was not fair to her to let her wonder what he had seen in his vision and worry about it all day.

"I really did crash up on the ridge, didn't I?"

"Yes. Is that what you saw?"

"Yes. I was flying the plane when it came down through the trees. I was alone in the airplane."

"Did you see anything else?"

"No," he replied with a disappointing sigh.

"Would you rather stay here?" she asked. "We could have a picnic out back of the house under the old oak tree."

"No. I would like to find a place where we can just enjoy a peaceful and quite afternoon together."

Becky smiled, but it was a forced smile. She was too worried about him for it to be a very happy smile. Pulling the reins to one side, she turned her horse and started across the lane toward an open gate.

Matt followed along behind until they had passed through the gate and out into an open field. He gently nudged the horse and moved up beside her as they rode out into the meadow.

After crossing the meadow, they rode along the edge of the woods, partially in the shade of the large trees. The valley was wide open and the spring flowers were in bloom. There was almost no breeze in the long narrow valley. The meadow was full of birds and colorful flowers of all kinds. With the recent rains, the grass was thick and green.

Near the end of the valley there was a creek with crystal clear water flowing slowly out into the valley. Becky turned her horse and headed up along the stream into the woods with Matt close behind her. Their horses walked along a narrow trail that ran near the edge of the stream. The birds were singing in the trees and the water was gently splashing over the rocks as it flowed down toward the valley.

The trail was not steep, but it was a fairly steady climb that wound around large boulders and trees. The narrow trail wondered away from the creek from time to time, but always seemed to find its way back. The shade of the trees provided protection from the hot sun as well as making it seem as if they were a thousand miles from civilization.

Suddenly, they broke out of the trees into a clearing. The ground was covered with a thick carpet of lush grass. The clearing was about two acres in size and located at the bottom of a shear rock cliff. The creek fell over the cliff making a beautiful waterfall and forming a small pool at the bottom. The creek flowed from the pool off down the hillside. The clearing was surrounded by big trees making for a very quiet and peaceful place.

Matt gently pulled his horse to a halt as he sat in the saddle and looked around. He never would have thought that there could be any place like it in the whole world. It simply invited a person to stop, breathe in deeply and enjoy its tranquility.

Becky stopped, dismounted and stood quietly beside her horse as she watched his reaction. By the look on his face, it was easy for Becky to see that it was just what he was looking for, and probably needed. She had always been able to forget about her problems when she came up here.

"This is beautiful," Matt said with amazement as he got off his horse.

"I think this is the most beautiful place in the world. Would you like to spend the afternoon here?"

"Yes. Yes, I would," he replied as he continued to take in his surroundings.

"We can lay the blanket out over here and use the saddles to rest our heads on," Becky suggested.

Becky took the saddle off her horse and placed it on the ground just a few feet from the pool. She then took the bridle off her horse and let the horse slowly wonder off. The horse walked off a few feet and immediately began to graze on the thick rich grass.

"Don't we need to tie them up, or something?"

"No. Bessy's been up here many times. She likes it here as much as I do. As long as she doesn't go anywhere, Samson won't either."

Matt was not too sure about that, but then they were her horses and she should know them. He took the saddle and bridle off Samson and let him wander off with Bessy.

"I wondered if the horses had names," he said as he set the saddle on the ground next to hers."

"My father got those two at a local auction about five years ago when they were just foals. I named them myself."

"Do you come here very often?" Matt asked as he continued to gaze around, impressed by the beauty of his surroundings.

"Not as often as I would like. You are the first person I've ever brought here."

She almost wished that she had not offered him that small piece of information. Yet, she did want to share her special place with him. It was difficult for her to understand her own reasoning. There were a number of places on the farm, or in the mountains that she could have taken him without bringing him here. By bringing him here, she had openly shared a part of herself that she had not shared with anyone else, not even Billy Joe.

Matt looked at her face as he walked up in front of her. He stopped, put his hands on her narrow waist and gently pulled her to him. She placed her hands on his shoulders and tipped her head back as he leaned down to her. Their lips met in a soft gentle kiss.

Becky could feel the warmth of his kiss through her entire body. It made her heart race and her knees feel weak. No one else had ever had such an effect on her. Even though she knew in her heart that it was not a good idea to get involved with him, she could not help herself. He made her feel alive, warm inside and loved. The strange part was that he had not chased her. He had made it a point to be careful not to get involved, until now.

Matt suddenly straightened up and pulled back away from her. He could see the hurt look in her eyes as if he were rejecting her. Without his past, he could not let himself fall in love with her. Yet, he knew that it was too late. He had already fallen for her.

"I better get some wood for a fire," Matt said as he removed his hands from her waist.

Becky turned her back to him and moved over by the saddles. She bent down and untied the blanket. Tears began to fill her eyes. She could not face him right now. She did not care about his past. She simply cared about him. It was no longer a matter of what was right or wrong, or what she should or should not do. She loved him and she could not help herself.

Matt watched her for a second as she busied herself spreading out the blanket. He wanted to go to her, take her in his arms and tell her that he was sorry, but he could not do it. It was going to be hard enough to leave her when he found out who he was, and if he had a family somewhere.

As Matt turned and headed toward the edge of the woods, Becky turned around and watched him walk away. She wished that she could say something to him that would make everything all right, but what could she say that would really help?

He was in love with her, and she knew it. With so much uncertainty and doubt, and so much missing from his past, she was convinced that he was afraid to show her how much he loved her. To get involved with him would simply make their parting more painful, but right now she didn't care.

Matt gathered dry branches from the ground until he had his arms full. It gave him time to think about Becky. She was in love with him, but why? She knew nothing about him, not even his name. For that matter, he knew nothing about himself. He liked the idea of being here with her. He wanted nothing more than to be here with her and hold her in his arms. He knew that when he had to leave, it would be very hard for both of them. Something deep down in the recesses of his mind told him that he would have to leave, sooner or later.

He returned to where Becky had laid out the blanket and dropped the wood. As he knelt to arrange the wood to build a fire, he looked over at her lying on the blanket. He did not mind at all that she was watching him.

Becky watched him, but did not see what he was doing. He was handsome and caring; he was gentle and kind, especially to her. It was clear to Becky that he was doing his best to avoid doing anything that would cause her pain.

She rolled over on her back and looked up at the clear blue sky. They had all afternoon together, she thought. She would accept what little time they had together. If it was the last day they could share, then it would have to be enough. The only other thing she wanted was for him to take her in his arms and hold her.

As soon as the fire was going good, Matt put the potatoes in the fire to cook. He waited for awhile, then put the corn in the fire. When it was about time, he unwrapped the steaks and put them on a small wire grill over the fire.

It was not long and they were enjoying an excellent meal, complete with wine. The fine food, the quiet of the beautiful small clearing, the soft breeze and the warm sun would have made for a perfect day. It was an almost perfect day, marred only by their fear of getting too close to each other. It was a closeness that they both wanted, but were afraid to share with each other. It was clouded by the fact that they knew that it would eventually cause them pain.

CHAPTER TEN

Becky was kneeling next to the creek rinsing off the plates while Matt was kneeling beside her in the sand scrubbing the soot and grease from the grill. She looked over at him and watched him as he worked. He seemed to be so engrossed in what he was doing that she wondered what was going on in his mind. Was he thinking about her, or was he too busy cleaning the grill? Was he trying to remember his past, or was he thinking about his future? There was only one way for her find out.

"What are you thinking about?" she asked softly.

Matt turned and looked at her. He hesitated for a few seconds before responding while he tried to put his thoughts in some kind of order. How was he going to tell her that he liked being with her when in all probability there was another woman in his life? What would it be like for her if he found out that he already had a wife?

"I was just, - - ah, - - thinking about this place," he said, afraid to tell her what was really on his mind.

"What about it?"

"It's so peaceful and quiet here. I really wish I could stay here, forever."

Becky turned away and looked off across the creek toward the woods. She could not look at him as her eyes filled with tears again. The tone of his voice, and what he said, made it clear to her that although he loved her, he was convinced that there was someone else in his past. Someone that he had once cared about very much.

Matt had a good idea what was going on in Becky's mind, but he did not know what to say to make it easier for her to accept and understand. Not talking about it was not the answer, but telling her what she already knew was not going to help, either.

He rinsed off the grill, stood up and took it over to the saddles. Sitting down on the blanket, he wrapped his arms around his legs, leaned forward and put his chin on his knees. The struggle going on within him was not helping him to remember, nor was it helping him to cope with his feelings for Becky. In fact, it made him feel as if he would rather not remember his past at all.

Instead, he felt that he would like to start over from right here, right now. He wanted to take Becky in his arms, hold her tightly and kiss her until all thoughts of his past went away, but that was impossible. He knew that his past would not go away. It could never go away until he learned what was hidden in his past.

Becky turned around and saw him sitting on the edge of the blanket. She stood up, walked up behind him and knelt down. Reaching out, she put her hands on his shoulders and began kneading the muscles of his neck. She could feel the strength in his shoulders, but she could also feel the tension in them. She wanted to wrap him in her arms until all his fears and doubts disappeared.

It was difficult for her, but she seemed to get a hint of what he must be going through. She still could not understand how hard it must be for him, but she knew that she was not making it any easier. She had fallen in love with him when what he really needed was someone to just be there for him.

"I'm sorry," she whispered. "What can I do to help you?"

"Maybe, we should go back to the house," Matt suggested reluctantly.

Becky gave out a sigh of disappointment as she sat back on her heels and looked at his back. The last thing she wanted to do was to return to the house. She wanted the day to be special for them, and it still could be. It could very well be their last day together. She did not want to waste it.

"Why can't we stay for just a little longer?" she pleaded.

Matt shrugged his shoulders, stood up and walked a few feet away from her before stopping. He closed his eyes, tipped his head back and let out a deep sigh. Tipping his head down and looking at the ground in front of him, he tried to gather his thoughts as best he could. He could think of several reasons to leave the place, but he could think of only one very good reason to stay, Becky.

Becky did not get up. She stayed on the blanket watching him while she waited for an answer to her question. She knew that she was making things difficult for him, but she could not help herself. It was becoming difficult for her, too. She loved him as much as he loved her. Why was it so hard for him to see that?

Matt turned around to face her. He was ready to tell her that until he knew more about himself, he would not let himself fall in love with her. When he saw the hurt look in her eyes, his head yielded to his heart and he said nothing. All he wanted to do was to take her in his arms, hold her and kiss her until the hurt went away. He was torn between taking her in his arms and walking away. At that point, he did not know what to do.

Becky wanted to believe that if they really loved each other they could make it work, no matter what the obstacles. But as she watched him try to deal with it, she knew that he was right. Returning to the house would be the safe thing to do, and probably the wise thing to do.

Until he knew who he was, and something about his past, his past would always haunt them. It would always be a wedge between them that would drive them apart and keep their love from becoming whole and complete.

"You're right, we should go back to the house," Becky finally conceded as she stood up.

Matt watched her as she moved off the blanket, turned her back to him and began rolling up the blanket. He wanted to stop her and tell her that he was wrong; but he had already convinced himself that no matter how much it hurt, it was the right thing to do.

After Becky rolled up the blanket and tied it to one of the saddles, she picked up one of the bridles and walked toward her horse. Bessy stood quietly as Becky walked up to her and put the bridle on her. It was as if the horse knew that it was time to go home.

Samson was on the far side of the clearing near some large oak trees. Matt picked up the bridle and started toward him. Suddenly, there was the deep throated roar of a mountain lion. Samson bolted and ran across the clearing as panic took control of him. Matt stepped in front of the horse and waved his arms in an effort to stop it, but the mountain lion had frightened the horse so badly that Matt had to jump out of Samson's way or be run over.

Becky had managed to keep a tight grip on Bessy's reins as the horse reared and danced nervously. Although Becky's horse was frightened, it did not panic and try to run. Matt ran to Becky's side as she tried to calm her horse.

"Are you okay?" she asked.

"Yes. Are you?"

"I'm fine."

Matt looked around. He was concerned about where the mountain lion had gone. Was it still just inside the woods, or had it run off, too? Keeping a watchful eye, he stayed at Becky's side as they led Bessy back to where the saddles had been left.

"Shouldn't we go after Samson?" Matt asked.

"No. He knows the way home. Once he settles down, he'll go back to the barn."

"Do you think that's the mountain lion that injured your other horse?"

"Probably. We don't have a lot of them around here. We had better get back to the house. Samson will probably get back before we do. Dad will worry when Samson returns without us."

Matt gathered up everything and put it in the saddlebags while Becky saddled Bessy. While he was putting the grill in the saddlebag, another flash from his past ran through his mind. He tried his best to understand what his mind had revealed to him. It was a door with the name of a company and the name of the president of the company on it. He did not understand what the company had to do with him, but it had to fit into the puzzle somewhere. He wondered if he worked at the company, or if he had been there recently for some reason.

Becky noticed the look on his face while he was bent over one of the saddlebags. She had seen that look several times in the past few days and she knew what was happening to him. It was difficult for her to stand there and wait for him to get over it, even though it lasted only a few seconds. She wanted to help him, but there was nothing she could do for him. She also realized that with each flashback, he would gain a little more insight into his past.

Matt turned and looked up at her standing next to the horse. He forced a smiled as he stood up.

"Another vision," he commented without further explanation.

"We'll leave that saddle and those saddlebags here. We can come back for them later. We can ride double back to the house."

"Won't the cat chew them up?"

"I don't think so, at least not before we can get back. When Samson took off, the cat probably heard us and took off in the other direction. They try to stay clear of humans."

Without any further delay, Becky swung into the saddle. She took her foot out of the stirrup and reached down to help Matt. He put his foot in the stirrup, took hold of her hand and the saddle, and swung up behind her. He wrapped his arms around her. As soon as he was ready, Becky turned Bessy back toward the trail and nudged her along. Bessy followed the narrow trail back down the hill toward the valley below.

Matt hung onto Becky as the horse plodded along. It gave him time to think. He knew that no matter what he found out about himself, the woman in front of him had changed his life forever. Even if he found out that he was married to the most wonderful woman in the world, Becky would always haunt his memories. She would forever be in the back of his mind. She would be the yardstick that he would use to measure all other women.

He gave a great deal of thought to Becky and what she meant to him. He wondered if the fact that she had saved his life was the reason that he felt the way he did about her. Maybe, it was the fact that she was so beautiful. It could be that she seemed to care about him a great deal that made him desire and love her.

As he thought of her, and all she had done for him, he was sure that there was no one reason for his feelings for her. It was a lot of reasons when put together became the reason he had fallen in love with her. His feelings for her were going to be the reason that it was going to be so hard for him to leave her. He knew deep in his heart that the day would come when he would have to leave. It was just a matter of time.

Becky could feel the strength in Matt's arms. It was not that he was holding her all that tightly, but just a feeling she had about him. She liked having his arms around her, even if it was to ride back to the house.

She could not help but think that Matt would most likely be leaving. That was the thought that continually haunted her. It was only a matter of time before he would either find out who he was, or he would figure it out for himself. She was convinced that when that happened, it would be over for them. He would return to his life with his family and loved ones somewhere else, and leave her to wonder what happened to him.

She would have liked to think that they could have some happiness together even after he found out who he was, but she could not allow herself to think that way. To hope for happiness with him would only lead to disappointment and unhappiness. If she did have hope, it would make it harder for her to give him up. It was easier for her to accept the darker side of things, than to accept the brighter side. The more she thought about it, the more she was convincing herself that there was no bright side for them.

As Bessy stepped out into the valley and turned toward the barn, Becky looked up the valley. She could see a white car parked in front of the house. It was too far away to see clearly, but there was no doubt in her mind that it was Sheriff Frank Stevens's car. Her heart sank and she slouched down in the saddle. Sheriff Stevens would tell him his name, where he was from and that would be the end of it. She was sure of it.

Matt could feel the slight slouch of Becky's body. He squeezed her slightly as if he was trying to support her.

"What's the matter?" he asked.

Becky took one hand and placed it over his hands. She wanted to turn around and go back into the woods to keep him from finding out who he was for just a little while longer, but that would be selfish of her. She could not do that to him no matter how much she wanted to keep him to herself.

"I think the sheriff's at the house," she said, the words almost choking in her throat.

He looked over her shoulder and saw the white car in the distance. It was going to be a difficult time for both of them. He had not really expected the sheriff to return so soon. He was not ready to say goodbye to her. He wanted to know who he was, but at the same time he did not want anything to change. He was beginning to like it here, and he liked being with Becky.

As they rode up to the fence and stopped, Sam came running over to them. Matt slid off the horse and reached up to help Becky down. Once on the ground, he took her by the hand as they walked toward the gate.

"What happened? Samson came home almost an hour ago."

Becky could see Sam's concern on his face and heard it in his voice, but she could also see Sheriff Stevens leaning against his patrol car, waiting and watching. It seemed to her that he was staring directly at Matt. She was sure that he knew something.

"A mountain lion frightened Samson where we were having our picnic. He panicked and ran home," Becky explained without taking her eyes off Sheriff Stevens.

"Are you all right?"

"We're fine. We'll have to go back and get the saddle and saddlebags," Matt replied with a forced smile.

Matt looked away from Sam toward Sheriff Stevens. The smile on his face faded away. He was reluctant to talk to the sheriff, almost afraid of what he might find out. Yet, it had to be done. Until he found out about himself, he was more or less in a state of limbo. It would be impossible for him to make any plans for his future until he knew about his past.

Matt let his hand slide out of Becky's as he started toward the house. Sam slipped his arm around his daughter as they followed Matt. Sam was also afraid of what the day might bring Becky. He knew that his little girl had fallen in love with Matt, and would be deeply hurt when he had to leave.

"Hi, sheriff," Matt said as he stuck out his hand.

"Hi."

Sheriff Stevens shook Matt's hand, all the time watching his eyes.

"Did you find out anything?"

"I don't know. I don't have the report on your fingerprints back, so that has not been much help, yet. It also seems that there are two planes missing as a result of that one storm. As best we can figure it, both planes went down within about forty miles or so of here. Apparently, the one you were in, and another small airplane that we have not been able to locate, yet.

"We know that the two planes carried only one person each, the pilots. We also know the name of only one of the pilots. It appears that you are one of them, but we don't know which one.

"Does the name Jeffrey M. Richardson, or Jeff Richardson, mean anything to you?" the sheriff asked as he watched Matt's face very closely for some kind of a reaction.

Matt thought as hard as he could, but the name meant nothing to him. If it was his name, it did not trigger any kind of a response.

He looked back up at the sheriff and shook his head. "No, sheriff. The name doesn't mean a thing to me."

"Well, as soon as we get the name of the other pilot, or the report on your fingerprints, I'll be in touch with you."

"Ah, this Richardson, what do you know about him, anything?" Matt asked.

"Not much. It seems that the police in Lima, Ohio have been trying to locate his wife to get a photograph of him, but she is out of town. It seems that he was to give a speech in Virginia, but never arrived. The people who reported him missing could only give the local police a very general description of him."

"Do I fit that description?"

"Like I said, it was very general and could fit thousands of men, including you. It's just not enough to go on."

Becky's heart sank. The thought that he might be Richardson, and the fact that Richardson was married, shook her deeply. As long as there was a possibility that he was Richardson, there was little hope for them to be able to stay together. It would not be easy for her to let him go, but she had nothing to say about it. There was nothing she could do but wait until they found out more information.

Matt looked over at Becky as she turned away and went into the house. The hurt look in her eyes pulled at his heart, but there was nothing he could do about it. He wanted to follow her and comfort her, but what could he possibly say to her now. If he was Richardson, he had a life somewhere else and staying here could only cause her more pain and disappointment.

"Sheriff, maybe I should go back into town with you."

"Okay, but I thought you were doing so well remembering little pieces of your past."

"I was, but maybe it's time to go on into town."

"Okay," the sheriff agreed.

"Now that you are strong enough, I was thinking we would go up to the site of the crash tomorrow morning. If you could see the plane again, it might jog your memory a little," Sam suggested.

Matt looked at Sam, then at the sheriff. It was a long shot at best, but it was probably all he had going at the moment.

"I think Sam might have something there. Maybe, seeing the plane will help. What have you got to lose?" the sheriff asked.

"Well?" Sam asked.

"Maybe your right. I'll stay," Matt agreed reluctantly, after all he had nothing more to lose.

"Good. Besides you have to go get my saddle back," Sam said with a smile.

Matt forced a smile, but he still had some serious reservations about staying. He said goodbye to the sheriff and went into the house to look for Becky while Sam talked with Sheriff Stevens on the front porch.

CHAPTER ELEVEN

Matt went into the living room looking for Becky, but she was not there. She was not in the kitchen, either. Stopping at the stairs, he looked up and wondered if she might have gone to her room. He went up the stairs and found the door to her bedroom open. Looking into her room, he saw her lying on her stomach across her bed with a pillow tucked under her. He hesitated to disturb her, but he needed to be near her. He walked into the room and sat down on the edge of the bed.

Slowly, she turned and looked up at him. Her eyes were red from crying and her cheeks were covered with tears.

"Are you okay?" he asked softly.

He wanted to reach out and wipe the tears away, but the look in her eyes made his heart ache for her.

"Are you Richardson?" she asked, her voice could hardly get the question out.

"I don't know for sure, but I don't think so."

She rolled over on her back and looked up at the ceiling, still clutching the pillow to her breasts. Her head was filled with thoughts, but she was having a difficult time sorting them out. If he is not Richardson, then who was he?

"I thought about going into town with the sheriff, but decided to stay here, at least until tomorrow. Your father suggested that I go up to the crash site with him tomorrow and see if it helps me remember anything."

"Are you going?"

"Yes."

"Do you think it will help?"

"I don't know, but I guess it's worth a try."

"Can I go with you?"

"I would like that," he replied with a smile.

Becky sat up on the edge of the bed beside him. She reached over and took hold of his hand. Just the idea of spending another day with him seemed to help lift her out of the deep depression that she seemed to find herself in.

"Your father said that I had to go back and get his saddle and the bags that we left behind. I'm not sure that I could find my way back alone. Would you be my guide?"

"Yes, yes, yes," Becky replied with a smile.

"Then let's go," Matt said as he stood up and reached out for her.

Becky reached up and took hold of Matt's hands. He pulled her to her feet, but did not let go of her hands. The smile faded from her lips as she looked into his eyes. He leaned down toward her. She tipped her head back and closed her eyes. At that moment, it did not matter to Becky who the man was. The feel of his soft warm lips as they touched hers was all she needed to know about him. That, and the fact that she loved him.

Matt looked down at her. As she opened her eyes, he could see the love in them. Right now, he wanted her more than he wanted to know his own name, but it was not the time or the place. If only they had met under different circumstances things might be very different, he thought. He wasn't sure what those circumstances might be. He let go of her hands, turned and started toward the door.

"Wait!" Becky said to him.

Matt stopped, but hesitated to turn around. Slowly, he turned and looked at her. He wanted to go take her in his arms and tell her that he was sorry, but he could not move.

"It's still early. We could take swimming suits along and go for a swim before we come back," she suggested.

Becky was not sure how he would react to her suggestion, but she wanted to spend what was left of the day with him. She could see that he was mulling it over. She knew that the more time they spent together, the harder it would be when it came time for him to leave. But, she could not help herself. She had him here with her now, and she had no intension of wasting what little time she had with him.

"I would like that," he replied softly, giving in to her wishes.

"I'll get what we need. I'm sure dad has a swimsuit you could wear."

Matt stepped in front of her and kissed her on the forehead, then turned and left her room. As he came to the bottom of the stairs, he almost ran into Sam. He stopped in his tracks and looked at Sam. There was something going on in Sam's mind, and Matt wondered what it could be. It was clear that Sam wanted to speak to him about something important.

"Is she going with you?" Sam asked.

"Sir?"

"Is Becky going with you to get the saddle?"

"Oh! Yes, she is."

"I don't know who you are, but I consider myself a pretty good judge of character. I don't think you are this Richardson fellah the sheriff mentioned."

Matt wondered what Sam was getting at. He had already come to the conclusion that Sam was not the type of man to beat around the bush about anything.

"I believe you to be a straight forward sort of fellah, the kind that wouldn't take advantage of others and wouldn't intentionally hurt anyone."

"Thank you," Matt said still trying to figure out what it was Sam was trying to say.

"I don't want to see my Becky hurt, do you understand?"

"Yes, I understand. I don't want to hurt Becky, either."

Matt understood all right. Here was a father who was worried about his little girl even thought she was a grown woman. Matt guessed that most fathers feel that way about their little girls, no matter how old their little girls are.

Just then, Becky came down the stairs and found Sam and Matt standing at the bottom. It was obvious that they had been talking about something serious. She looked from one to the other trying to figure out what they had been talking about.

"What's going on here?" she asked.

"We were just having a little man-to-man talk," Sam replied.

She smiled at her father and put an arm around him. It was not hard for her to figure out what her father had been doing. It was not the first time that Sam had a man-to-man talk with one of her boyfriends.

"I'm not a little girl any more. I'm a big girl and I can take care of myself."

"I know you can, honey," Sam said as he leaned over and kissed her lightly on the cheek.

"We better get going," she said as she handed the canvas bag to Matt.

Matt turned and walked through the living room and out the front door with Sam and Becky following along behind. Becky still had her arm around her father when they stepped out onto the porch.

"What time do you think you will be home?" Sam asked.

"We'll be home before dark," Becky answered.

"You have a good time, and keep an eye open for that cat."

"We will. We'll keep the horses close by this time."

"Good. Have a good time."

Sam stopped on the porch. Becky took her arm from around him, gave him a kiss on the cheek, and then ran to catch up with Matt. When she caught up with him, she took hold of his hand as they walked the rest of the way to the paddock.

"You'll have to forgive my father, he worries about me," Becky said as they walked through the gate.

"I don't blame him. He loves you very much," Matt replied as he closed the gate behind them.

Becky stepped up to Samson and put a bridle on him while Matt watched. He was not sure about riding the horse bareback. When Becky finished and turned to look at Matt, he just smiled.

"We'll ride double on Bessy," she said with a smile.

Matt let out a sigh of relief. He reached out and took the reins as he handed the canvas bag to Becky. She hooked the bag over the saddle horn, then mounted up.

After handing the reins back to her, Matt put his foot in the stirrup and swung up behind her. He wrapped his arms around her waist, and they started off down the meadow with Samson following along behind.

Sam watched them as they rode off. He wanted to protect his little girl from any harm, but she was right. She was no longer his little girl. She was an adult, which entitled her to make her own mistakes. All he could do now was to be there when she needed him, and hope that she did not hurt too much when Matt had to leave.

* * * *

As they came into the clearing, Matt looked around for some sign of the cat, but he saw none. He slid off the horse and held Samson's reins while Becky dismounted. The saddle and bags where right where they had left them, untouched.

Becky looked around and found a couple of short, but fairly heavy branches lying on the ground. She tied Bessy to one of them. The branch was heavy enough to discourage Bessy from going very far, yet not so heavy that it would prevent her from grazing near the pool.

Matt had watched how Becky had tied Bessy and he did the same to Samson. He then picked up the saddle blanket and saddle and threw them up on Samson's back. At least that way if Samson decided to run for home, he would be taking the saddle with him.

After having watched Becky saddle a horse, he was sure that he could do it himself. After he was finished and was sure that he had secured the saddle properly, he asked Becky to check it. He did not want the saddle to come loose, especially while he was on it.

"Would you mind taking a look at this?" he asked.

She smiled as she walked over to him. She had been watching him as he saddled Samson.

"Very good. We'll make a horseman out of you, yet," she said with a smile.

"Shall we go for that swim?" Matt asked.

"Sure. I'll go change."

He watched as she took her swimsuit from the canvas bag and went behind a large clump of bushes. While she was changing, Matt laid out the blanket close to the edge of the pool.

"It's your turn," Becky said as she came out from behind the bushes.

Matt turned, looked up and observed her as she approached him. He had known that she was a beautiful woman with a very nice figure, but in her dark blue one piece swimming suit, she was gorgeous. The deep V cut neckline showed off the soft tan of her skin and the round firmness of her breasts. The snug fit of the suit also showed off the smooth flowing lines of her body and the shapeliness of her hips and long legs.

Becky dropped her clothes on the blanket and smiled as she watched Matt admire her. She knelt down in front of him.

"Are you going to change?"

"Ah, - - yes."

After handing him a swimsuit from the canvas bag, Matt got up and walked over behind the bushes. Within a few minutes, he returned carrying his clothes. He dropped them on the blanket next to hers.

Becky had watched him as he came out from behind the bushes and found him to be very handsome. He had broad shoulders, strong muscular chest and arms, and a narrow waist. Except for the remainder of some black and blue marks on his shoulder and one side of his chest, he was healing very well. Good color had returned and he once again had a healthy tone.

He stood looking down at her as he reached out to her. She took hold of his hands and he pulled her to her feet. Without a word, he led her out into the crystal clear water of the pool.

The pool got deep quickly and it was not long before they were waist deep in the cool water. They knelt down in the water and pushed off the bottom. Using the slow easy movement of the breaststroke, they swam across the pool toward the rocky cliff and the waterfall.

As they swam up to the cliff, Matt reached it first and discovered that there was a ledge about two or three inches below the surface of the water. The ledge ran along the base of the cliff and was about three feet wide. He turned around and sat down on the ledge, while he waited for Becky to catch up.

Becky saw that he had found the ledge and swam over to him. She turned around and sat down on the ledge beside him.

"Does this ledge go over there under the waterfall?" he asked.

"I don't know; but if it does, it would make a good place to take a shower."

"Let's find out," he suggested.

He stood up on the ledge and held his hand out for her. She reached out and took hold of his hand. He pulled her up in front of him.

"You first," Becky said.

Matt smiled at her, let go of her hands, turned around and began slowly feeling his way along the ledge. With the sun glaring off the rippling water, it was very hard to see the limits of the underwater ledge. He could feel the warmth of Becky's hands on his shoulders as she carefully moved along behind him.

He worked his way along until he was under the small waterfall. It felt good to have the cool water pour over him. He turned around, took hold of Becky's hands and gently pulled her under the waterfall with him.

She let go of his hands and tipped her face up. She let the water wash over her as she pushed her hair back away from her face and back over her shoulders. The cool water felt good against her skin. As she looked back at him, he reached out and put his hands on her hips.

She reached up and put her hands on his shoulders as he pulled her close to him. As her body began to press against him, she let her hands slide around behind his head and wrapped her arms around his neck. She could feel the warmth of his chest through her swimsuit as her breasts pressed against him.

Their lips met in a warm passionate kiss. Matt slid his arms around behind her and pulled her tightly against him. Her body pressed hard against his. The open back of her swimsuit allowed him to slide his hands over the soft smooth skin of her back.

The passion of their kiss was only slightly cooled by the clear water falling over them. As their kiss came to an end, Becky laid her head on his shoulder as she tried to catch her breath. She could hear the solid sound of his heart beating and feel the rise and fall of his chest as he tried to regain his breath.

She wanted to tell him that she loved him and that no matter what they found out about him, it would not make her love him any less. The warmth of his hands on her back gave her a secure feeling. The last thing she wanted was for the moment to end.

Matt could feel her breath on his shoulder as he held her. He could not believe that he could possibly love anyone as much as he loved the woman in his arms. But even that thought could not erase the thought that there might be someone out there in the world that he had once loved as much as he loved her. Was it possible that there was someone out there that loved him as much as she loved him? Right now, he did not think so, but he could not remember anyone else.

That question confused Matt more than he would like to have admitted. Tomorrow might provide the answer. If a hike up to the crash site helped him regain his memory, it might also end what they could have together. Yet, they could not really have anything as long as he could not remember his past. It was sort of a catch 22.

With that thought, Matt reluctantly let go of Becky. He looked into her eyes as he gently, but firmly pushed her away.

She looked at him as she took her arms from around his neck. His reaction and apparent rejection confused her. She could not figure out what was going on in his mind. One minute he was gentle and loving to her, the next he was distant and aloof. At first she thought that he may be having another one of his visions, but his reaction was completely different.

Matt turned away from her and looked out over the water. Without a word, he dove off the ledge and out into the pool. He swam down deep, his mind full of conflicts that he could not seem to resolve. In his heart, he knew that he was going to hurt Becky because he did not belong here. He almost wished that he had gone into town with the sheriff. It was not the life he had led before he lost his memory, he seemed to know that, but it was a life he would like to live.

Becky watched him as he came up and swam toward the other side of the pool. She could not understand what had made him dive off the ledge and leave her. She was sure that he had not had another vision. Maybe, he just did not want her, but she did not believe that for a single second. Maybe, he was afraid of what he might find out about himself. That, she decided, was entirely possible. It was also something that she could understand.

She wanted to follow him, but instead she moved out from under the waterfall and sat down on the ledge. Maybe, it was time for them to step back and look at what was happening to them, she thought.

CHAPTER TWELVE

Becky watched Matt closely as he lay on the blanket on the other side of the pool. She wondered what was going through his mind. If he loved her as much as she loved him, not knowing his past must be tearing him apart inside. Not knowing if he had a girlfriend, a fiancée, or a wife hidden away in his past had to put a lot of pressure on him.

She knew that their feelings for each other were not making things any easier for him, but then it was not easy for her, either. It had never been her intention to fall in love with him, or to have him fall in love with her. It just happened, and there was nothing either of them could do about it.

Matt looked up at the clear blue sky. What was wrong with him, he silently asked himself. He had done the one thing that was not only stupid, but would cause pain to someone that he cared about very much. He had convinced himself that it was his fault that Becky had fallen in love with him. He should have seen it coming and put a stop to it before it got out of hand. But how was he to stop it? Love could not be stopped. He knew that because as hard as he tried not to fall in love with Becky, he still had fallen for her.

He knew that it was too late to worry about that now. It was time to figure out what to do about it. He thought about simply moving into town until he found out who he was, but that would not solve anything. It would only hurt them both knowing that the other was only a few miles away.

He thought about telling her some story about himself as if he had just remembered who he was, but he did not like that idea any better. He even considered telling her that he had never really lost his memory at all, and that the whole thing had been a lie from the beginning. But he knew she would see though that, too.

The more he thought about it, the more he realized that he loved her too much to hurt her even more by not telling her the truth. He felt that it was time that they faced the facts straight on. If he sat her down and told her everything he knew about himself and how he felt about her, they might be able to come to some kind of an understanding, at least they would both know what to expect.

His thoughts were interrupted by the sound of a splash in the pool. He sat up and looked off across the pool. Becky was slowly swimming across the pool toward him. He watched her as she walked out of the water and stood in front of him.

She was beautiful. The sun sparkled off the droplets of water on her skin. She had pushed her dark hair back away from her face and it gently cascaded over her shoulders. The smooth flowing lines of her body were accented by her swimsuit. The sad look in her beautiful brown eyes was the only thing that distracted from her beauty.

"I'm sorry," she said in almost a whisper.

"What have you got to be sorry for? I'm the one who should be asking you for forgiveness."

She knelt down on the blanket beside him and he handed her a towel. As she wiped the water from her face, she quickly tried to put her thoughts in order. What could she say to him that would make sense?

"Becky, I love you," he blurted out before she could say anything.

She slowly moved the towel from her face and looked at him in disbelief. They had both tried so hard to avoid any expression of their feelings for each other that his sudden admission of his love startled her. It came as a complete surprise. It was not the fact that he loved her that was the surprise, but the fact that he admitted it to her.

The surprised expression on her face gave Matt cause for concern. He was sure that she knew that he had fallen in love with her. Her reaction to his statement confused and worried him.

"Did I say something wrong?" he asked, afraid that he might have frightened her with his admission of his love for her.

"Oh, no. It's just - - ah - - I - ah." She stopped trying to find the words to explain her reaction to him. As she looked at his face, a smile slowly replaced the surprised look on her face.

"I love you, too," she said as she leaned forward and threw her arms around his neck.

He let out a sigh of relief as he wrapped his arms around her. Slowly, he laid down on his back and drew her over him. He had not planned to express his love for her, but it just sort of popped out. It was clear to both of them that it had needed to be said.

Their lips met in a hard passionate kiss. He rolled over on his side taking her with him. They broke off the kiss and looked into each other's eyes as if trying to see who loved who more.

Becky smiled at him as she rolled off him. She curled up against his side and laid her head down on his shoulder, resting her arm across his chest. For the first time she felt that there was no problem so great that they could not overcome it.

"I can't give you any guarantees about the future. I don't even know what is going to happen tomorrow, let alone next week or next month," he said in an effort to make her understand the uncertainty of their future together.

"I know," she replied softly.

At that moment, it was enough for Becky to be at his side. She was content to share what little bit of time she had left with him. Tomorrow would have to wait until tomorrow.

"I don't even have any idea what Sheriff Stevens might find out about me."

"I know," she replied as she snuggled up closer to his side and curled a leg over him.

"I might be married," he said reluctantly.

His last comment gave her reason to pause. She had to think about that for a minute. Slowly, she rose up and looked at him. It was clear that he was having a great deal of difficulty trying to deal with the situation without knowing everything that might enter into their relationship. She wanted so much to make it easier for him, but how? She had to say something that would calm his fears and make him realize that she understood.

"I don't even know your name, but I know that I love you. I know that there are no guarantees in life. I know that life can be cruel. I know that to live life, you have to take some risks. I understand all that," she said as calmly at possible.

"Under normal circumstances, I would agree that you understand. But these are not normal circumstances. I don't even know who I am," he argued.

Becky had listened to every word he had said. The words told her that he was warning her that it was not a good idea to get involved with him, that there was too much uncertainty, too much at risk.

In her head she had to agree with his assessment, but her heart would not let her agree. The way his hand rubbed gently on her shoulder as he spoke, the way he tucked her up against his body, and the soft breaks in his voice as he talked to her; told her that his heart did not agree with his head, either. It also told her that he did love her. All he was trying to do was to prepare her for the worst, whatever it might be.

"I didn't know who you were before that plane crashed on the ridge, but that doesn't matter. I fell in love with the man who has been living in the same house with my father and me for the past few days," she said in a slow, clear and concise manner.

She was trying to make her point as clear as possible, maybe in an attempt to convince herself as well as Matt. She was feeling as unsure of herself as he must have been.

"I don't know if you were any different before the crash, but that does not matter. I don't know what's in your past that we may have to deal with in the future. What I do know is that we can deal with anything that comes our way if we really want to."

"You make it sound so simple."

"It's not simple. Oh God, it's not simple," she said as a tear came to her eye. "We just have to deal with whatever comes along, when it comes. We can't second guess everything. If we try, it will drive us crazy; and we will never know what we could have had together.

"Just how we deal with it will depend on how we perceive it, how important it is to us."

Matt had to admit that she could put up a pretty strong argument. It was clear to him that she was a lot stronger than she appeared. If she wasn't, she certainly could put up a terrific front. The major question in his mind was, is she strong enough to handle it if he finds out that he is already married. He suddenly realized that he had to ask himself that very same question.

Becky did not wish to discuss what might happen any more. There were already too many unknowns for them to come up with any kind of a solution, so further discussion would resolve nothing at that point in time.

Becky was not even sure she really believed everything she had said, but she wanted to believe it. If she did not believe that they had a chance to build a lasting, permanent relationship, she was asking for nothing but heartache and more pain.

"I love you and I want you to kiss me, right now," she said in an effort to lighten things up a bit and change the subject.

"Right now?"

"Yes. Right now."

"Okay."

Matt wrapped his arms around her and rolled her up over him. Sliding one hand behind her head, he pulled her down to him until their lips met.

It was a hard kiss that grew in passion faster than either of them had expected. She moaned softly as their lips parted and their kiss grew deeper.

She could feel the warmth of his body through her swimming suit as her breasts pressed hard against his chest. The touch of his hand slowly sliding down her to the small of her back sent a sensation through her entire body. She could not seem to get close enough to him even though she was laying on him with the full weight of her body over him.

He could feel the firmness of her breasts against his chest and the warmth of her skin under his hands. As their passion grew, his heart raced and his breathing became more rapid.

Becky rose up again and looked down at him. Her eyes showed the love that was in her heart for him. A soft smile came over her lips, and then she laid her head down on his shoulder. She could feel his chest rise and fall with each breath he took, and she could hear the rapid beating of his heart. For just a few seconds, he was hers and hers alone. There were no thoughts of others.

It was painful for her to think about what might happen once he found out about his past. She wanted to hope for the best, but it seemed almost too much to hope for. As much as she would like to push those thoughts out of her mind, they just would not go away for more then a brief moment at a time.

Matt let his hand gently slide over her back without giving it a single conscious thought. His head was filled with thoughts of Becky. She was the most giving person he had ever met, but then he could not remember meeting very many people. He wondered if it was possible that he might have loved someone else as much as he loved her.

His thoughts were disturbed when Becky rolled off him and curled up at his side again. He liked the feel of her soft hand as she gently touched his chest and the feel of her fingers as she lightly ran them over the outline of the bruises on his shoulder.

She slowly rolled over on her back and looked up at the sky for a minute. Why did she have to have so many complications in her life? Why couldn't they just be allowed to fall in love and be left alone? Life could be terribly cruel sometimes, she thought. She turned her head and looked at him. A smile came over her face.

"Kiss me," she said softly.

The soft tone of her voice let it be known that it was neither a question nor a demand, but rather a loving request. Matt rolled onto his side, propping his head up on his hand.

Becky's dark brown eyes sparkled in the sunlight. Her long dark hair framed her softly tanned face. Being wet, a lock of hair clung to her forehead. Matt reached up and carefully pushed it aside. He leaned down over her until their lips met again.

It was a much softer kiss. A kiss with the feeling of their deep love for each other that went clear to their souls.

As Matt rose up a little and looked down at her, his desire for her was almost uncontrollable. He could see that she was having similar feelings.

Just as he slid his hand up her side and over one of her firm breasts, a bright flash of light passed before his eyes and his breath caught. It startled him and he sat up quickly. A vision of his past suddenly came to him, intruding on their moment.

It startled Becky, too. The suddenness of his vision and his reaction frightened her. She reached out and touched him, but he did not respond to her touch. The look on his face caused her to think that he might be in a great deal of pain and gave her reason to be alarmed.

It was the first time she had seen him with so much pain on his face. It seemed to her that the vision lasted longer, much longer than the others. She quickly realized that there was nothing she could do for him except to hold him and wait for it to pass. She sat up and knelt behind him. Wrapping her arms around him, she laid her head on his shoulder and held him tightly.

The vision was very strange to him. There was the same woman in the vision that he had seen in a vision a few days earlier. The woman was screaming at him for some reason he could not understand. The woman suddenly slapped him and motioned for him to leave. He could envision himself turning and walking out the door into another room that seemed to have no connection to the room he had just left. In the room was another woman who smiled at him and seemed to be talking to him very pleasantly.

Just as suddenly as the vision had come to him, it was gone. He blinked his eyes and turned to look at Becky. He could feel the sweat running down his face and he was breathing hard.

"Are you all right?" she asked.

That simple question brought him back to reality. Their love would never have a chance if they tried to run and hide from his past.

"Yes," he replied between short, deep breaths.

"You had another vision, didn't you?"

"Yes."

"Tell me about it."

"I saw two women. One was yelling at me and slapped me across the face. The other smiled and seemed to be very nice to me. I don't understand what's happening or what it all means."

She squeezed him and continued to hold him in her arms in an effort to comfort him. It was all she could think of that might help him in his time of confusion. She hated to see him in such confusion. Each time he had a vision, it seemed to take just a little more out of him, and seemed to take him a little longer to get over it. It also made her feel that he was slowly being pulled away from her by someone in his visions.

As Matt regained his breath, she let go of him. He turned around and sat back on his heels. He looked into Becky's eyes and could see the hurt that the incident had caused her. At that moment, it was easy for him to comprehend that there could be no future for them until he knew about his past. No matter how much they loved each other, not knowing about his past would always come between them.

"I think we should go back to the house," Matt said with a sigh of disappointment.

Becky was beginning to feel that Matt was not telling her everything, that he was leaving little important parts out. She did not want to go back to the house, not yet. What she wanted was for him to talk to her, not shut her out. She wanted him to tell her everything he could about his visions, all his visions. She didn't know how, but maybe she could help him understand them.

She hesitated as she looked at him, but decided that she would do as he wished. If he did not want to talk about it, she would not try to force him.

Standing up, she gathered her clothes and a towel. She looked down at him for a second, then turned and went behind the bushes to change.

Matt watched her as she disappeared behind the bushes. He felt the need to talk to her, but what was he going to tell her. 'I can't love you because I have two other women in my past?' As long as he could not put the pieces of the puzzle together for himself, how was he going to explain any of it to her?

While she changed, she had time to think about what he had said. She knew in her heart that he was not sharing himself completely. Why wouldn't he share what he knew about himself with her? Why was he holding back? Was it possible that he knew a lot more about his past than he wanted to admit? By the time Becky returned, she had worked herself up to a point where she was very upset with him.

Matt had the blanket rolled up and tied to one of the saddles. He then went behind the bushes to change. When he returned, he saw Becky sitting up on Bessy, apparently ready to go. He stuffed his wet suit and towel in the canvas bags, hooked it over the saddle horn and mounted Samson.

She briefly glanced over at him and saw that he was ready to go. She wished that he had been as ready to share himself with her as he was to go, but apparently that was not the case. Without a word, she turned her horse and gently nudged Bessy along. The horse slowly started back down the trail. As Becky rode past him, she looked straight ahead and said nothing.

Matt nudged his horse and began following her. Just as he was leaving the clearing, he looked back. The place was going to hold a lot of memories for him that he would not easily forget. He wondered if he would ever see it again.

CHAPTER THIRTEEN

The horses with their riders moved slowly down the trail to the meadow below. The sun was shining through the trees casting shadows along the trail and on the surrounding bushes causing a beautiful array of colors among the wild flowers. It was still warm, but a slight cool evening breeze began to make its way through the trees.

Matt had been watching Becky closely as he followed her. Her long brown hair shone in the sun as it bounced gently with each step of her horse. Her back was as straight and as rigid as a steel rod.

He wanted to stop her and talk to her, to tell her everything that he knew about himself, everything that frightened him and everything he felt, but he was afraid. But what was he afraid of? Why couldn't he tell her everything he knew about himself? She had been at his side every step of his recovery and deserved to know everything about him that he could remember. She had nothing but love and understanding for him. She was there for him, even without having to ask her.

He ran all his fears and concerns through his mind as if reviewing and examining each one carefully. If he truly loved her, there was no reason for him to hide anything from her. If she truly loved him, she would at least try to understand what little he knew about himself. It was time for him to share with her everything he knew about himself, even if it didn't make any sense to him right now. He needed to trust her if there was to be any possibility of them having any kind of a solid relationship.

As they came out of the woods into the meadow, Matt nudged Samson up along side Bessy. He looked at Becky, but she continued to look straight ahead, trying to ignore him. It was only then that he realized how much he had hurt her by not sharing himself completely with her. It was time to remedy the situation.

"Becky, I need to talk to you."

She turned and glanced at him briefly, then turned back to look straight ahead. There was fire in her eyes, but he could not blame her for being upset and not wanting to talk to him.

"Please. I need to talk to you, please," he pleaded.

"Okay," she replied as she pulled back on the reins causing Bessy to stop quickly.

"Would you mind if we walked for awhile?" Matt asked softly.

Matt did not wait for a response. He dismounted and walked around in front of his horse. Looking up at Becky, he waited for her to dismount and join him on the ground. He could see that she did not seem to want to get down off her horse, but she finally gave in and dismounted.

He tried to smile as she joined him in front of the horses. Without saying a word, he began walking slowly up the meadow toward the house. She walked silently beside him, waiting for him to speak to her.

"First of all, I want you to know that I love you very much."

Becky turned and looked at him for a second. She thought about saying something sarcastic like 'you really know how to show it', but decided that it would only make matters worse. After all, he was trying to talk to her and that was what she had wanted all along.

Instead, she just looked down at the ground in front of her as she walked and listened.

"I have had several visions, recalls, flashes; whatever you want to call them. I don't know what they mean, except the ones where I crashed the plane. This is very hard to explain."

"I'm listening," Becky said softly in an effort to get him to continue.

"I have had visions of two very different women. One seems to be rather short with blond hair and blue eyes. She seems to be friendly and caring. I don't know who she is, or what she could possibly mean to me.

"The other woman is taller, I think, and also has blond hair. She always seems to be yelling at me and is always angry with me. She even slapped me once. I don't have the slightest idea why she hit me or why she seems so angry all the time."

Becky listened very carefully as he continued to tell her about the women in his visions. Her mind filled with anxiety. Her first thought was that one of the women was most likely his wife. She almost wished that the woman who was always yelling at him would be his wife. If she were, he might consider leaving her.

"I also had a vision of an office," he continued. "It was an aviation business of some kind, I think. There was a name on the door."

"Can you remember the name?" she asked as she looked over at him.

"Yes. I think so. I think it was Matthew Steward."

Becky stopped and turned toward him. Matt also stopped and looked at her.

"Are you Matthew Steward?" she asked as she looked into his eyes.

"I don't know. I could be, I guess. I just don't know. I don't feel the same way about the name as I did about the name, Richardson."

"What do you mean?"

"It's kind of hard to explain. I just didn't feel that Richardson was my name when I heard it, but Matthew, or Matt Steward doesn't give me that same kind of feeling. I'm just not sure."

Becky reached out with her free hand and took Matt's hand. Again, they started to walk up the valley toward the barn. She thought about the name of Matt Steward and wondered if the sheriff had found out the name of the other missing pilot.

"Have you been able to put any of the visions together?" Becky asked.

"No, not really. About the only thing I can figure out is that I might have something to do with an aviation company. After all, I was flying a plane and I did see an aviation company in one of my visions. I know that's pretty thin."

"At least it's a start."

"Sure it's a start, but to where? Where am I from? And what about the women? Am I married to one of them? Maybe, one of them is my wife, or possibly my ex-wife. Maybe, one of them is a girlfriend, or possibly a secretary or something. I still don't understand that part yet," Matt said with a note of frustration.

Becky squeezed his hand hoping he would know that she would be there for him. She did not know what to say to him that would help relieve some of his frustration. It was probably better if she just walked quietly beside him and listened.

"It's hard not being able to remember your past, but at least you make it easier for me to deal with it," he said as he looked at her and lightly squeezed her hand.

"I'm glad," she replied as she looked up at him.

"Thank you for listening to me," he said as they stopped at the back door of the barn.

They stood gazing into each other's eyes for several seconds before Matt let go of her hand. He reached out and put his hand on her hip. She moved closer to him and put a hand on his shoulder. He leaned down as she tipped her face up to meet him. Their lips met in a light, tender kiss.

When the kiss ended, Becky smiled up at him. Taking her hand from his shoulder, she turned and led her horse through the door and into the barn. Matt followed her horse through the door, leading Samson into the barn.

It was fairly dark in the barn as the sun was about to set. Matt was distracted by the beautiful woman in front of him. She had been so patient and loving toward him.

Suddenly, out of the corner of his eye, he saw something coming out of the darkness. Before he could react, whatever it was struck him on the side of the face. He saw a bright flash of light, and then there was darkness again. Sharp pain ripped through his jaw and cheek. He felt his legs buckle as he started to fall backwards, slamming into the wall. Deep in his darkness, he heard Becky scream, but his brain was so fogged by the sudden jarring of his head that he could not make out what she was saying or what was happening.

"NO!" Becky screamed as she turned around and saw him falling to the floor.

She dropped the reins and rushed to Matt. She knelt down beside him and took him in her arms. It was not clear to her what had happened as she had her back to him when she heard him fall against the wall. In the dim light of the doorway, however, she noticed that there was blood on one side of his face. She quickly realized that he had been hit on the side of his face with something.

Becky heard something move behind her and quickly turned to see who was there. She saw Billy Joe as he stepped out of the shadows and into the light of the doorway. He was rubbing his knuckles. From the sadistic look on his face, she realized that he must have hit Matt when Matt was not looking.

"You bastard," she screamed at Billy Joe.

She could not remember a time when she had felt so much hatred for anyone in her life. There was nothing she could do about Billy Joe right now as Matt needed her help. She took her neckerchief and began wiping the blood from Matt's face.

"You get away from him," Billy Joe said as he reached down and took Becky by the arm.

"Let go of me," she yelled as she twisted her arm loose.

"I said, get away from him," he said angrily as he reached down and grabbed her by the arm again.

Billy Joe dragged her across the dirt floor, away from Matt. Once she was away from Matt, he jerked her to her feet. As he turned her around, he let go of her. Standing between her and Matt, he began slowly moving toward her, forcing her to back away from him.

"You'd better stop, Billy Joe," she warned him.

Becky did not yell at him. She knew that he had a quick, violent temper, but she could not remember ever seeing him so enraged. It was clear that Billy Joe had lost all control of himself.

"I'd better stop? You'd better stop. Don't you know that he could be dangerous? He could be a killer, or something worse," he said as he took another step closer to her.

"Oh really, then what are you?"

She continued to slowly back away from Billy Joe as he slowly moved toward her. He frightened her and she wanted to keep her distance. She had never been so scared in her life, but not just for herself.

Suddenly, he reached out and grabbed her by the arms. With a swift jerk, he pulled her up against him and looked down at her. He was squeezing her arms so hard that it hurt, but she did not let out a sound.

"You have become a slut. The city has made you evil. You don't even know him and you let him kiss you. I used to love you, but you are nothing."

Billy Joe pushed her away hard and she lost her balance. She fell backwards hard against one of the stalls. The sudden impact knocked the wind out of her and she fell to the dirt floor.

As she lay on the floor, she gasped to catch her breath.

"You want to take another swing at me?"

Billy Joe turned around quickly to find that Matt was leaning against a stall about ten feet away. He looked him up and down, but did not consider Matt to be any kind of a threat. After all, he could hardly stand up without leaning against something.

As Billy Joe started to move toward Matt, Matt straightened himself up and looked Billy Joe in the eye. A slow nasty grin came over Billy Joe's face. Matt was sure that Billy Joe would have no trouble taking him in a fist fight, but he could not let him beat up on Becky without putting up some kind of a fight.

"If you don't want to leave this barn with a bunch of holes in yeah, yeah damn well better leave now," Sam said in a very quiet, yet forceful voice.

Billy Joe stopped in his tracks and slowly turned around. Standing less than six feet from him was Sam with a pitchfork firmly gripped in his hands. Sam had moved around so he was standing between Billy Joe and Becky, and had those long sharp prongs pointed right at Billy

Joe's stomach. Billy Joe knew Sam well enough to know that when it came to his daughter, there was nothing Sam wouldn't do to protect her, including putting a bunch of neatly spaced holes in him with the pitchfork.

"Okay, okay, I'll go," Billy Joe said as he raised his hands in surrender. "But this isn't over."

"It better be over, or you'll live just long enough to regret it," Sam countered, the anger in his voice showing that he meant business.

Sam did not make any move to let up on his demand for Billy Joe to leave. He kept the pitchfork pointed at him. Billy Joe walked well out of Sam's reach as Sam followed him to the barn door. He did not take his eyes off Billy Joe until he was out of the barn and well on his way down the road.

As soon as Billy Joe was out of the barn, Becky got up and ran to Matt's aid. She wrapped her arms around him to give him support as she helped him to a bale of straw where he could sit down.

"Seems I've been here before," Matt said in an effort to lighten things up a little.

"We better get him in the house," Sam suggested.

Together, they helped Matt to his feet. With one on each side of him, they walked him to the house and into the kitchen. Becky got some water while Sam went for a first aid kit.

"I'm all right," Matt said as Becky wiped the blood from his cut lip causing him to flinch.

"Are you sure?"

"Yes. He caught me by surprise, but that won't happen again," he assured her.

"I don't think he will be back," Sam said as he returned to the kitchen. "How are you feeling?"

"I've felt better, I think."

"Why don't you two go out on the porch and relax. I'll fix you something to eat after I take care of the horses."

"Sounds good to me," Matt said.

"Me, too," Becky agreed.

Matt stood up and reached out a hand to Becky. She took his hand and walked with him to the porch. He sat down on the swing at the end of the porch and she curled up beside him, tucking her legs up under herself. He wrapped his arm around behind her neck, resting his hand on her shoulder.

"Your father's a great guy."

"Yes, he is."

"I wish I could remember what my father was like."

"You will, someday," she said softly trying to reassure him that everything was going to be all right.

That simple statement made her feel sad, but it helped her realize how important the little things in life should be. She laid her head on his shoulder and wondered if he had been so gentle a man before the accident. She had heard that a person often changes after an accident that almost takes their life.

Matt gently caressed her shoulder as he looked off toward the paddocks. It was so peaceful and quiet here. The thought of staying here even after he regained his memory passed through his mind.

It didn't take Sam long to unsaddle the horses and stable them for the night. He returned to the house and fixed a light dinner. He carried a tray with three glasses of milk and a large plate of sandwiches out onto the porch.

After setting the tray on the table, he sat down in a lawn chair next to it.

"Dinner is served."

"Sandwiches for dinner?" Becky asked.

"Sure, why not? You had a steak dinner with all the trimmings for lunch, didn't you?"

"Yes. Yes, we did. Sandwiches are fine with me," Matt replied with a smile.

The three of them sat and ate while they listened to the crickets. It was going to be a beautiful night. There was a gentle breeze coming down the valley that was just enough to keep the mosquitoes away.

After dinner, Sam took the dirty glasses and the tray inside, leaving Matt and Becky alone on the porch swing. It was so quiet that neither of them wanted to break the silence. They simply sat on the swing and enjoyed their time together.

It was getting late when Sam stepped out on the porch to say goodnight. After he had gone inside, Becky rested her head on Matt's shoulder.

"I think we should go in, too," she said not wanting to go inside, but it was getting late and they had a busy day scheduled for tomorrow.

Matt had to agree. It had been a rather trying day, and it would do him good to get some rest. He took his arm from around her neck and waited for her to get up. Standing up in front of her, he reached out and put his hands on her shoulders.

She reached out and put her hands on his hips as he drew her close to him. Tipping her head back to look up at him, she waited for him to kiss her. As their lips met, she let out a soft sigh. She liked it when he kissed her and held her close.

He let go of her. Slipping his arm around behind her, he walked her to the door. Once inside, they walked to the stairs together. At the bottom of the stairs, he turned her toward him, took her in his arms again and held her as he kissed her goodnight.

Reluctantly, he let her go and watched her as she went up the stairs to her room. As soon as she was out of sight, he went back into the living room. After removing his clothes, he laid down on the sofa where he had been sleeping. He laid there for a little while thinking about the day. No matter what seemed to happen, Becky was there for him. His thoughts of her were what made his life seem just a little more complete. In just a few minutes, he was sound asleep.

Becky went into her room and undressed. She lay down on her bed, pulled the covers up and closed her eyes. It took her a few minutes to fall asleep as her mind was filled with thoughts of Matt.

CHAPTER FOURTEEN

Becky lay quietly in bed and listened to the sounds of the early morning before opening her eyes. The birds singing in the tree just outside her window, the soft rustle of the leaves and the faint whinny of a horse in the paddock had been the sounds that she had grown up with. They were the very sounds that she had missed while living in the city.

She could feel the soft gentle breeze drift into her room and brush lightly across her sheets. The morning air smelled fresh and felt cool against her bare skin. She opened her eyes, and saw the sun was shining in, casting soft shadows across the foot of her bed. It was so peaceful that she did not want to get out of bed, not just yet, anyway.

Her thoughts immediately turned to last night when Matt had kissed her so tenderly while they stood at the bottom of the stairs. Her heart fluttered as she thought of him. She liked the way he made her feel when he held her in his arms. She rolled over and wrapped her arms around one of her pillows, clutching it to her breasts as she fantasized about what life could be like with Matt.

Her pleasant and dreamy thoughts were suddenly invaded by the thought of the two women that Matt had described to her. It was not possible for her to think of Matt without thinking of the two women that kept coming into his visions.

In her heart, and in her mind, she was sure that one of them was going to make her very unhappy. She did not know how or even when, but she had already convinced herself that it would happen.

Tears came to her eyes as she thought of the two women. She would lose him to one of them because he would feel that it was his duty to return to where he came from. At first she had been willing to accept what little time they had together, but it was different now. They loved each other, and she did not want to give him up.

It was clear that their love for each other was going to be tested, tested in a way that only the strongest love would be able to survive. It was a test that she did not want to happen. It saddened her heart to think that she might not be able to pass the test that would allow him to stay with her.

As her thoughts gradually turned to today, she remembered that they were going to go up on the ridge to where the airplane had crashed. In a way, she did not want to go. If he found out who he was, he would leave that much sooner. She knew that she was being selfish, but she could not help how she felt. Even though she did not want to go up on the ridge, she knew that she could not let him go up there without her. No matter what the outcome, she had to be with him.

"Hey, sleepyhead. Are you going to get up?"

Her thoughts were suddenly interrupted by her father's voice as he called her from the bottom of the stairs. She smiled to herself as she had heard him call her like that so many times in the past.

"I'm awake. I'll be down shortly," she called back.

"You better or you'll miss breakfast."

"I'm coming."

"Wear something comfortable. We're climbing up to the ridge this morning."

"I know, I know," she whispered as she pushed the pillow off to one side and sat up.

The sheet slid off the smooth lines of her body as she stood up and walked across the room to the bathroom.

After finishing in the bathroom, she dressed in jeans and a light denim blouse, not the dressiest thing she could find, but very practical for the climb. She slipped on a pair of heavy socks and her hiking boots. After lacing up her boots, she took a quick look in the mirror and decided that she was ready for the hike up the ridge, as ready as she would ever be.

"Good morning," Matt said as Becky came into the kitchen.

"Morning," she said shyly. "What's for breakfast?"

"Bacon, eggs, toast and coffee," Sam replied.

"That sounds good," she said as she pulled up a chair.

She glanced across the table at Matt. It was difficult for her to look at him, but she forced a slight smile. All she could think about was that today was the day that she would most likely lose him. It seemed that it would almost be easier if she kept her distance.

Sam set a plate down in front of her. He watched as she stared at the meal for several seconds before she reached for a fork. He had a pretty good idea what was going on in her head. He could feel the tension in the air. Watching the two of them together, it was clear that his little girl had fallen pretty hard for this stranger, who had literally dropped out of the sky and into her life.

"You look very nice this morning," Matt said softly.

"Thank you," she replied.

Becky looked back at her plate and began to eat. She was not very hungry, but with the hard climb up to the ridge she would need a good breakfast.

"I've packed a lunch. I figured that the two of you might want to make a day of it."

Becky looked up at her father with surprise. She thought that he was going with them, but now she was not so sure.

"Aren't you coming along?" Becky asked.

"No, I don't think so. I have a lot of things to do around here."

"Are you all right?" She worried about her father. After all, he was not a young man any more.

"I'm fine. I just thought that the two of you would like to spend the day without me tagging along. I expect the sheriff will be by sometime later today. Someone should be here to keep him company until you two get back."

Matt looked at Becky, then at Sam. He liked the idea of spending the day with Becky, but if Sam knew the sheriff was coming by, the sheriff must know something.

"Shouldn't I be here when the sheriff comes? He might have some information about me?" Matt asked.

"Sheriff Stevens and I have been friends for a very long time. If he has any news about you, he will be more than willing to wait until you get back."

"If we wait until the sheriff comes and he doesn't have any news, we will have wasted the whole day. If we go, you might find out something important about yourself," Becky added, hoping that she could convince him to spend the day alone with her, a day that could very likely be their last day together.

Matt looked at Becky. His head told him that he should wait and see what the sheriff might have found out. But no matter what his head told him, he wanted to spend as much time as possible with Becky. If he could spend just a few more hours with her, he would not let it slip away.

"I suppose you're right, but...," Matt said.

"You two go ahead and go. Take your time. If you find out something about yourself, all the better. If you don't, what's the loss? If the sheriff has any news, what difference will it make if you hear the news at two o'clock or four o'clock or even at eight?"

"I guess it wouldn't make any difference," Matt agreed after thinking about it. "A few hours one way or the other won't matter much."

Becky suddenly felt relieved. Her resolve to keep her distance had been shattered when she first saw him sitting at the table, but it was okay with her. She was going to be able to spend one more day alone with him. It was going make it harder for her to let him go when the time came, but right now she was not about to let the chance to be with him slip away. She was going to seize the moment.

"I have your backpack right here," Sam said as he set it down on the table in front of Matt. "It has sandwiches, some fruit, some leftover fried chicken and something to drink. Oh, there's a blanket in the pack, too."

"Thanks, Daddy," Becky said as she stood up.

"Your welcome, honey."

Matt picked up the backpack as he stood up. He swung it over his shoulder and walked to the back door to wait for Becky.

"Now you kids be careful. If it starts getting dark before you come down, hold up someplace. It's too rough up there to try to travel at night."

"We'll be careful," Becky said as she joined Matt at the door.

"You lead the way. I'm afraid I don't remember the trip down the mountain," Matt said.

Matt slipped the backpack on as they walked side by side to the edge of the woods. Becky stepped into the woods and Matt moved in behind her as they started up the narrow trail that would take them to the top of the ridge.

Becky found the trail to be a lot easier to travel. The rocks were not wet or slippery, and the leaves were dry making for much better footing.

Matt was finding the trail to be a little more difficult than he thought. He had gained a lot of his strength back, but apparently not enough for him to push hard up the side of the mountain. He found himself gradually falling behind.

"I think you are going to have to slow down a little. I'm not used to this kind of exercise. At least I don't feel like I am."

"I'm sorry. Would you like to stop and take a break?"

"Maybe, just a short one."

Becky looked around and saw a tree that had fallen. She led the way to it, and they sat down on it so he could catch his breath.

"I don't know how you ever got me down from up there," Matt said as he looked around.

"It wasn't easy, but we had the advantage of wet ground, and we were going down hill. When the ground gets wet up here, it gets very slippery."

Matt reached out and took her hand. Looking into her eyes, he said, "Just in case I forget to tell you, thank you."

"You're welcome," she replied and leaned toward him.

Matt leaned toward her until their lips met in a soft, tender kiss. As he pulled back and looked into her eyes, she smiled softly.

"Well, you ready to push onward and upward?"

"Sure," he said.

Matt stood up and pulled Becky to her feet. He held her hand for a second before she turned and started to move past him. Once again, she led the way toward the top, only now she was moving along the trail a little slower.

As the time went by, the sun moved higher into the sky. It had gotten quite warm by the time they reached the top of the ridge and found the outcropping where her father had seen a part of the plane before. When they broke out of the trees into the light, they discovered just how much the trees had protected them from the heat. Standing on the outcropping they could see for miles across the thick forest that covered the Allegheny Mountains.

"This is the most beautiful sight I have ever seen," Matt said.

Becky stepped up beside him and slipped her arm around behind him. She did not say anything, she simply watched him as he took in the sight.

The sky was a beautiful royal blue with only a few fluffy white clouds slowly floating across it. The hillsides below were a dark rich green with several gray rocks jutting out here and there. It was so peaceful and quiet up on the ridge.

Suddenly, Matt stopped looking around and focused on one spot. Several hundred yards below and to the right was an area that did not seem to fit in with the surrounding landscape. There was a path where the trees appeared to have been knocked down, and there was a large dark spot in the middle of the vast green forest.

"Is that where I crashed?" he asked as he stared out over the hillside.

"Yes," she replied softly.

Becky watched him for some kind of reaction, but there was none. She wanted to say something, but she had no idea what to say that would mean anything to him. It was up to him now. There was nothing she could do, but stay close to him and wait. Wait until he was ready to go down there.

He took a deep breath and looked toward Becky.

"Shall we go?"

"If you're ready."

"I'm as ready as I will ever be. Lead the way."

Becky turned and moved back off the outcropping. She started down the steep slope with Matt close behind her. She would have liked to have had Matt walking beside her, but the woods were too thick and what little trail there was, was too narrow.

It was a difficult time for both of them. Matt seemed to be having the most difficulty. He was as much afraid of what he might find out about himself, as he was about what he might not find out.

It took close to half an hour before Becky found the path where the airplane had cut through the trees. The airplane would be only a few hundred feet further down the slope. She stopped and turned toward Matt. It was not hard to see the anxiety in his face.

"Are you sure you want to go further?" she asked.

"I have to," he replied as he looked into her eyes.

Becky said nothing more. She did not fully understand, but she understood enough to know that he really did not have a choice. She simply turned around and started toward the remains of the small airplane.

What they found was a shock to both of them. Matt had no idea what he would see as he had been unconscious, but Becky had not seen the remains of the airplane after the fire had burned out. They had left the area while it was still burning.

Before them, in the midst of the vast colorful forest, was the blackened shell of what was once a modern, state of the art aircraft. There were parts of the airplane spread about the area.

She stood there looking at the charred remains of the airplane. All she could think was that if they had been only a few seconds later, Matt would have been burned alive.

At the moment, she was wishing that she had not come up here at all. But when she looked over at Matt and saw the look on his face, she knew that she had to come here as much as he did. It was quite possible that their future, whatever it might be, was dependent on them coming here, together.

Matt took the pack off his back and set it next to a tree. He stepped up beside Becky and took hold of her hand. As he looked at the wreckage and the charred skeleton of his airplane, he realized the risk that she and her father had taken to save him.

The grass and a few trees close to the airplane had been burned, or at least blackened by the fire. It had been the heavy rains that had kept the fire from spreading to the surrounding forest.

Matt let go of Becky's hand and he began slowly walking around the airplane. He was looking for something, but he had no idea what he was looking for. Maybe, there was something here that he had to find. Something that might help him discover who he was, or where he was from. Possibly, it would be something that would help him discover something about himself.

He walked up close to the airplane and looked inside the cockpit. The fire had gutted the inside of the airplane. Only blobs of melted plastic, charred instruments and bits of metal twisted by the heat of the fire were visible. It was hard to believe that it had once been an up-to-date, top of the line airplane.

As he looked around, he discovered two metal latches from a briefcase that had been almost totally consumed by the fire. Everything that had been in the briefcase was gone. All that remained were the two small metal latches.

Becky stood back and watched Matt as he looked around. She noticed that he had picked up something from inside the airplane. It appeared to be a couple of pieces of metal of some kind, but she could not see them clearly. She wondered why he seemed to be examining them so closely.

"Did you find something?"

"I'm not sure," he replied.

He took one last look around the inside of the airplane before he turned around and walked back toward Becky. He stopped several times to look back at the airplane. In his hand, he still carried the briefcase latches.

"What do you have?"

"I think these are the latches from my briefcase," he replied as he continued to examine them with her.

She looked at him as if he had discovered something of great value. Glancing up at her, he wondered what was on her mind.

"Do you realize what you just said?" she asked.

"What?"

"You just said that those are the latches from your briefcase. How do you know it was your briefcase?"

Matt looked at her, then at the latches. She was right. How did he know it was his briefcase? It could have been anyone's briefcase, but for some strange reason, he was sure it had been his.

He wandered off away from the plane to a place where he could look out over the entire site. He sat down on a log and studied the remains of the airplane.

Becky walked over and sat down next to him. He was thinking so hard that she did not want to disturb him. She waited for him to break the silence.

"I was returning from a meeting in Richmond. I had just finished putting together a business deal and I was on my way back," he said more to himself than to Becky.

"The weather had suddenly turned nasty and I flew into a heavy thunderstorm. I tried to fly around it, but my plane was hit by lighting. I lost control of it and shortly after that I crashed here."

Matt stopped and looked at Becky. He realized that he had just replayed the events leading up to the crash, but there were still parts that he could not remember.

"Back to where? You said you were on your way back, back to where?" Becky asked, her excitement showing in her voice.

Matt thought for a minute, then turned to her. "I don't know."

"Who was the meeting with, do you remember?"

"I don't know that, either," he replied after giving it some thought.

"It's past noon. Why don't we rest here for awhile," Becky suggested.

"Okay."

Becky stood up and picked up the pack. She opened it and took out the blanket and spread it out on the grass under a large tree. As she laid out a couple of the sandwiches, she looked over at Matt. He was still staring at the wreckage. She wondered what must be going through his mind right now. He looked so tired, so weary. She was sure that the climb had not been easy for him, but it was more than that. Seeing the remains of his plane and remembering what had happened seemed to take a lot out of him, too.

"Come over here and eat, please. We can rest before we start back," Becky suggested.

Matt turned and joined her under the tree. After they finished eating, Matt lay down and put his head in Becky's lap. It was not long before he was asleep.

Becky ran her fingers lightly through his dark hair. She was very worried about him. Leaning back against the tree, she let out a sigh and closed her eyes. She whispered a small pray that all would turn out well for them, then fell asleep herself.

CHAPTER FIFTEEN

Becky woke with a start when she felt Matt's head move in her lap. Glancing down at him, it was easy to see that he was still asleep, but that he was very restless. He was mumbling something, but she could not understand what it was he was saying.

She lightly touched his forehead in an effort to calm him. As soon as she ran her fingers lightly through his hair, he seemed to settle down again into a more restful sleep. It caused Becky a great deal of concern. What could possibly be going through his mind that would cause him to be so restless? Was he having visions in the form of dreams while he slept?

She tipped her head back against the tree again, only she did not close her eyes and try to sleep. She looked out at the remains of the airplane and wondered. It was clear that he had been in Richmond, but she was still puzzled about where he had been going. It bothered her to think that he might have been returning to one of the women he had told her about.

She closed her eyes and tried to visualize what life would be like with him, but all she could think about was life without him. In her mind, she was certain that he would one day walk down the dirt road in front of her father's farm and never return. The thought of him leaving weighed heavily in her heart and on her mind. Even though he was lying with his head on her lap now, she was missing him already.

Matt opened his eyes and turned his head to look up at her. He noticed a tear had crept out from under an eyelid and was slowly rolling down her cheek. It was not necessary for her to tell him what was going on in her mind, he already knew. It was the same thing that haunted his mind every waking moment.

She opened her eyes as he sat up in front of her. Forcing a smile, she wiped away the tear.

He reached out to her and took her in his arms. With her arms wrapped around his neck, he held her close to him. He could almost feel the sadness within her as she buried her face against his neck.

Gently massaging her back, he turned his head and looked out at the charred airplane. He had come here with the hope of finding himself, but all it had shown him was how much he loved Becky. At the moment, the past did not seem all that important. What he wanted was right here in his arms.

Matt took her by the shoulders and gently pushed her back. He looked into her tear-filled eyes.

"I don't want to stay here any longer," he said softly.

"Are you ready to head back?"

The look in her eyes and the cracking of her voice told him that she was not ready to go back to the house, at least not yet. He was sure that the thought of returning to the house would mean that he would be leaving soon.

"No. I don't want to go back. I just want to get away from here," he said as he looked deep into her eyes.

"Where do you want to go?"

"I don't know. Any place where we can be alone. Some place where my past will not be watching us. Some place where you and I can be together."

Becky looked at his face. It was not difficult for her to understand what he was asking. She wanted it as much as he did.

After thinking for a moment, she remembered a place a short distance away. Like many secluded spots in these mountains, it was a quiet, peaceful place. A place she hoped would not be invaded by his past.

"I know a place."

"Good, let's go there."

Matt stood up and took hold of Becky's hands. He helped her to her feet. He knelt back down and rolled up the blanket. As soon as the backpack was ready, he stood up and put it on his back. He walked up to her and took her hand in his.

"Lead the way," he said with a smile.

Becky reluctantly let go of Matt's hand, turned and started off down a narrow path that led deeper into the woods. Matt started to follow a short distance behind, but stopped. He turned around and took one last look at the burned out shell of his airplane before he turned back and followed Becky along the narrow trail.

It did not take them very long to reach a small clearing at the bend of a creek. The clear cool water flowed out of the woods and on down the narrow valley, disappearing back into the woods. Except for the small sandy beach-like area on the inside of the bend of the creek, the creek was surrounded by thick green grass and shaded by large trees.

Matt took the pack from his back and laid it up against a large oak tree. He slowly looked around as he took in the quiet beauty of the secluded place.

"This is beautiful," he said as he looked around.

"The water is fresh and cool," she said as she watched him look around.

Matt strolled over to the creek and knelt down beside it. He splashed a little of the cool water on his face. It was refreshing on such a hot day. As he sat back on his heels, he turned and looked at Becky.

"I don't want to go back to the house tonight," Matt said quietly.

Becky looked into his eyes and she could see that he was pleading with her to stay here with him tonight. It was not a difficult decision for her to make, she wanted as much time with him as she could get. What better place to spend time together than right here.

"We have plenty to eat. I can make a small fire that will keep us warm all night," Matt added in an effort to plead his case for staying.

A soft smile came over Becky's face. "Am I going to need a fire to keep me warm?"

Matt's concerned look turned to a soft smile. "No, but a fire would be romantic."

"In that case, we should have a fire."

Matt stood up and walked up to Becky. He reached out and put his hands on her narrow waist as she reached up and put her hands on his shoulder. Gently, he pulled her up to him.

Becky tipped her head back as he leaned down to kiss her. When their lips met, she let her hands slide around behind his head and she held him to her. She moaned softly as their kiss deepened and her body pressed tightly against him.

Matt could feel the firmness of her body against him. He let his hands slide around behind her to the small of her back. As their passion grew, he slid his hands down over her firm behind.

Reluctantly, he pulled back and looked down at her. Her love for him showed in her clear, sparkling brown eyes. He may not know who the other two women he had seen in his visions were, but he knew who the woman was in his arms, and what she meant to him. It was impossible for him to imagine that he could love anyone else as much as he loved her.

"Maybe, I'd better get a place built for a fire."

Becky smiled up at him. "How can I help?"

"Would you like to help gather some firewood?"

"Sure," she replied as she took her arms from around his neck.

As soon as he let go of her, she walked to the edge of the woods. It took her a few minutes before she began gathering dry pieces of wood from the forest floor. Although she had kept control of her emotions while he held her, his kiss had penetrated to the very root of her being. Whatever the world had in store for them would simply have to wait until tomorrow. Tonight was going to be just for the two of them.

When she returned to the clearing with her arms full of wood, Matt had dug a shallow hole in the sand and surrounded it with rocks. He had already broken up a few branches and arranged them in the hole.

"Is it possible that you were a Boy Scout when you were younger?" she said as she dropped her bundle of wood near the fire pit.

Matt thought for a second before he answered. "I don't know. It's possible, I guess."

Becky went over to the pack and pulled out the blanket while Matt finished preparing the fire. She watched him as she laid out the blanket on the sand near the fire pit.

Looking into the pack, she noticed that there were still several pieces of chicken and a couple of sandwiches. There was also plenty to drink. She smiled as she thought of her father and how much he had packed for them. She wondered if he had planned it so that they would not have to return to the house today.

Becky got up and walked over to the creek. After splashing a little water on her face, she washed her hands. The water felt cool and refreshing on her skin. She glanced over at Matt and found him watching her.

"It feels good," she said with a smile.

Matt did not reply, he simply smiled and watched her as she returned to the blanket. He had everything ready for a fire. The fire was laid, the branches were all broken up to the right size and neatly stacked close to the fire pit. It was still too warm for a fire, and it would be several hours before the sun would set.

Becky sat down on the blanket and leaned up against a large log that had fallen some years ago. She sat with her hands behind her head, and her feet crossed in front of her. She watched him, almost studying him as he stood up.

After he got up, he walked over to the creek where he washed his hands. He took a minute to splash a little more cool water on his face. After he washed up a little, he joined Becky on the blanket, laying down on his back beside her and closing his eyes. He rolled over and laid his head on her lap.

It was a good time to just relax and be near him, she thought. She liked to have him lay beside her with his head on her lap. She looked out over the creek as she gently ran her fingers through his hair. She had to agree that it was just the place that they were looking for, quiet, beautiful and away from the rest of the world.

It was difficult for her not to watch him. There were a few drops of water still on his face that sparkled in the sunlight. The cut on his head was healing very nicely and did not appear that it would leave much of a scare.

Becky turned her head and looked up at the sky. As much as she wanted the rest of the world to stay away, she could not keep the thought of him leaving her from her mind.

As she watched a fluffy white cloud pass overhead, she said another silent prayer. She asked that he not have to leave her, that he could stay with her forever.

Looking back down at him, she caught him looking up at her. She felt a little embarrassed that he had caught her praying, but quickly realized that he could not have heard her silent pray.

"What's on your mind?" he asked softly.

"I don't know. Nothing, I guess." she replied with a deep sigh.

He rolled over on his side and reached out to her, touching her shoulder. "Please," he said softly.

She hesitated, but decided to tell him anyway. "I was thinking about you leaving."

"What about it?"

"I may never see you again."

"That will not happen," he said as he sat up.

"How can you say that? It will happen."

Becky pulled away from him and stood up. Looking down at him, she wondered how he could say a thing like that. It was inevitable that he would leave. The only thing that was not set in stone was when, or if he would ever return. Turning, she walked to the edge of the clearing and stopped. She wanted to run away so she did not have to face him, but she could not leave. Crossing her arms in front of her, she stood looking off into the woods. Tears began to roll down her cheeks.

Matt stood up and walked up behind her. He wrapped his arms around her and gently held her to him.

"I'll admit that I will have to leave for a little while to clear up some things, but I will come back. I promise," he said as he lightly kissed her on the neck.

"You don't know that. How can you be so sure?" she asked with a sob.

"I'm sure because I love you," he whispered.

She wanted so much to believe him, but her mind was full of doubts. Becky could feel the warmth of his breath in her hair, and his lips as he lightly kissed her neck just below her ear. She tipped her head to one side to make it easier for him to kiss her neck again.

The warmth and tenderness of his kiss slowly washed away her fears, at least for the moment. She moaned softly as he nuzzled the soft skin of her neck. Turning around in his arms, she wrapped her arms around his neck and kissed him hard. Pressing their bodies against each other, their passion grew rapidly as did their breathing.

She reluctantly relaxed her hold of him and leaned back to look up at his face. Only his eyes would be able to tell her if he really meant what he said. It was clear that his desire for her was as strong as hers.

"I need you here with me," he said breathlessly.

"I know," she replied in a soft whisper.

He once again leaned down and kissed her. He held her tightly, feeling her body pressed hard against him. He slid his hands down to the small of her back, and he held her as if to let her go would cause her to vanish like smoke in the wind. He hesitated to loosen his grip on her as their lips parted. He looked down at her and smiled.

"You are beautiful," he said softly.

"Thank you," she replied with a slight smile.

She slid her arms from around his neck as he took his hands from around her waist. They walked back to the blanket and sat down together. After taking off their boots and sox, they laid down. It was a good time to just be close to one another. She laid her head on his shoulder and curled up against his side. She felt secure in his arms as she listened to the steady rhythm of his heartbeat.

They lay there on the blanket for some time. The air was fresh and the slight breeze made the warm day more tolerable. The clear sky promised a very pleasant night, and the blanket they had would most likely be enough to keep them warm.

The sun was setting in the west and Matt was beginning to feel a little hungry. He did not want to disturb Becky, but if they did not eat soon they would be eating in the dark.

"Are you hungry?"

"A little," she replied as she rose up off his shoulder.

She sat up on the edge of the blanket while he rummaged through the backpack. They sat quietly on the blanket while they ate sandwiches and some chicken. By the time they had finished eating, the shadows had grown long and the light was fading fast.

Matt moved over near the fire pit, knelt down and started the fire while Becky packed up what was left of their food. A soft glow came from the burning branches. She knelt down beside him and put her arm around him. She watched him as he carefully added larger branches to the fire.

Becky's mind filled with thoughts of the two of them. With him beside her and the glow of the flames reflecting off his face, she felt that it was the way things should be for them. They belonged together.

The heat of the fire began to touch her skin. It had been hot most of the day, and she was feeling a little sticky from the hike up to the ridge. The thought of rinsing off the perspiration with a dip in the cool water of the creek was very inviting to her.

Without saying a word, Becky stood up and walked a little ways away from the fire to the edge of the creek. She stepped into the slow moving water near the edge. The water cooled her feet and felt good flowing over them. She stepped back onto the sandy beach. Reaching up to the front of her blouse, she slowly unbuttoned each button, pulling her blouse loose from her jeans.

Matt looked over toward Becky just as she slipped out of her blouse and dropped it to the ground. He did not move, but instead watched her as she took off the rest of her clothes, carefully dropping each item on the ground near her feet.

It was impossible for Matt to take his eyes off her. In the dim glow of the fire, he could see the smooth curved lines of her naked body.

Once she had removed all her clothes, she slowly waded out into the creek. At the deepest place, it was just barely up to her waist. She slowly bent down, lowering herself into the water until she disappeared under the surface. The cool water washed over her, rinsing the perspiration from her body. When she came up again, she tipped her head back and pushed her hair back away from her face.

Matt stood up and walked over to the edge of the creek. The glow of the fire on her face and on her firm breasts aroused his desire for her.

"Would you like company?" he asked.

He knew it sounded kind of corny, but she was so beautiful standing in the water that he could not think of anything else to say.

"Yes. I'd like that," she replied with a soft smile.

Becky did not move, instead she stood in the water and watched Matt as he took off his clothes and dropped them on the sand beside hers. She liked the sight of him as the glow of the fire accented his strong build. She thought that he was beautiful, too.

He waded out to her and stood in front of her, but he did not reach out to her. Instead, he lowered himself into the water until he disappeared under the surface. He quickly rinsed off the sweat of the day. After he came up and pushed his hair out of his eyes, he reached out to Becky and put his hands on her narrow waist.

As she stepped toward him, she slid her hands up over his chest, over his shoulders and around behind his neck. She tipped her head up and closed her eyes just as their lips met. She shivered slightly as her bare breasts brushed against his bare chest. His skin was cool from the water, but warmed quickly as she pressed her body against his.

She ran her fingers through the hair on the back of his neck as their passion grew deeper and deeper. She liked the feel of his hands moving slowly up and down her back. The feel of his hard body against her in the cool water made her desire him even more.

Matt ran his hands up her back. Her skin was soft and smooth to his touch. He pulled back slightly and looked into her sparkling eyes. It was hard to tell if the glow on her face was from their passion or from the glow of the fire.

"I want you," she whispered.

Matt bent down a little and scooped her up in his arms. She curled up against him as he carried her out of the creek to the blanket. He knelt down, laying her down on the blanket. He then lay down beside her. He lightly slid his hand up her side and over one of her breasts as he looked at her lying there beside him.

Looking into his eyes, Becky reached up and slid her hand around to the back of his neck. Slowly, she drew him down over her until their lips met.

The fire slowly burned down to embers as they made love. The quiet of the night and the warm night air allowed them to drift off in their own private world, undisturbed by the world that lay beyond their little piece of it.

CHAPTER SIXTEEN

The sun was just showing a hint of light in the morning sky when Becky opened her eyes. The cool morning air along with a slight breeze caused her to shiver. She rolled over and saw that Matt was laying on his side with his back to her. He had no covers over him. During the night, their blanket must have fallen down between them. She took a few seconds to look at him lying naked beside her. He looked so strong and handsome.

She reached down, pulled the blanket up and covered him with it. As she pulled part of the blanket over herself, she curled up against his back and wrapped her arm around him. She snuggled up against his back and kissed him lightly on the back of his neck. The warmth of his body against her made her feel warm and secure again. In just a matter of a few minutes, she was asleep again.

* * * *

The sun had cleared the tops of the mountains and was beginning to warm the lovers as they lay on the small beach. Matt opened his eyes and took in a deep breath of the clean mountain air, but laid still. He could feel the warmth of Becky's body against his back and her breath against the back of his neck. He was sure that she was still sleeping and he did not wish to disturb her.

He could not think of a more pleasant way to wake up in the morning than to be wrapped in the arms of someone who loved him. He loved her so much that he was willing to give up his past, whatever it might be, to stay with her.

After a short while, Becky began to move. She slid a hand over his chest as she snuggled the full length of her body against him.

"I love you," she whispered and kissed the back of his neck.

"I will give you all day to quit that."

"Oh, you will," she said teasing him.

"On second thought, maybe not," he said as he turned over and took her in his arms.

She quickly wrapped her arms around him as he rolled her up over him. Laying her head on his shoulder, she moaned softly as his hands stroked the smooth curves of her back. His touch was gentle, which was a stark contrast to the hard body under her. Being naked with him seemed as natural as the sun rising in the morning and setting at night.

No matter how hard she tried, having his hands touching her body could not completely keep her from thinking that their time together would have to come to an end soon. Maybe the time was so special for them because they were so sure that they would not have another chance to be together. That thought was very depressing for Becky and brought tears to her eyes.

Still lying on top of him, she rose up and looked down at him. The look on his face told her that he was having his doubts about their future together, too.

"Will you come back for me?" she asked in a soft whisper.

"Yes, I promised I would," he replied softly.

Slowly, she leaned down to him until their lips met. It was a long, loving kiss that was meant to reassure them that their love would be forever. But would it? No matter how loving their kiss, their love for each other might last forever; but would they be able to be together forever?

Becky rose up a little and rolled off Matt. He rolled onto his side and propped his head up on one hand. As she turned to look at him, he reached out and rested his hand on her stomach. Her skin was warm and soft to his touch.

She put her hand over his hand and held it to her. Becky smiled up at him as the thought that she did not even know his name passed through her mind. What had made her smile was the fact that she did not need to know his name, all she needed to know was what kind of a man he was. He was gentle and kind, he was considerate, and he was caring of her and her feelings. She knew of several people who would prefer to have a man like him, even without a name.

"I think we should get dressed and start back, don't you?" Matt asked, not convinced in his own mind that he was ready to go back.

"Yes. We should," she replied reluctantly. "But I would like to take a dip in the creek before I dress."

"May I join you?"

"Yes," she replied softly.

Matt leaned down to her until their lips met. As he kissed her, he gently slid his hand up over her firm breast. She held his hand against her breast and returned his kiss with the same passion as it was given.

Matt rose up and looked into her eyes. He wanted to stay right here with her, but knew that it was not possible. He forced himself to roll away from her. After he stood up, he reached down and took her hands. Helping her to her feet, he pulled her up in front of him. He hesitated for a second, then let go of one of her hands. They turned and waded into the creek without another word.

Once in the creek, Matt let go of her hand and lowered himself into the cool water. He ducked his head under the water to refresh himself and rinsed the sand from his body and hair.

Becky knelt down in the water beside him. She also ducked under the water to rinse the sand away. Pushing her hair away from her face, she laid down in the stream and let the cool water wash over her naked body.

Matt watched her for a minute, then decided to leave her alone with her thoughts. It was going to be a very hard day for her, he thought as he walked out of the creek to where they had dropped their clothes. He stood in the sun to let it dry him. As he dressed, he thought about her and how much he loved her. He also thought about how much leaving her was going to hurt.

After a short while, Becky stood up and walked out of the creek. She stood in the sunlight with her back toward him as she began dressing.

Matt watched the sun sparkle on the droplets of water on her skin as she dressed. As she buttoned her blouse, she turned toward him and saw that he had been watching her. She did not mind that he had been watching her.

"You are beautiful," Matt said.

"You are, too," she replied with a smile as she walked toward him.

Matt was kneeling on the blanket and looked in the backpack. He pulled out the last two sandwiches and held them up.

"I guess this is all we have for breakfast. These, and a couple of cans of pop."

"Well, if that is all we have, then I guess that will be our breakfast," she said as she knelt down on the blanket beside him.

Matt handed her a sandwich and a can of pop. He unwrapped the sandwich for himself and they began to eat. It was a time when they were each lost in their own thoughts of what the day might bring.

As soon as they were finished, they packed up the blanket and got ready to leave. Becky was about to point in the direction that they needed to go when she noticed that Matt had his hands over his eyes and his head was tipped down. She instantly knew that he was having another vision.

She moved close to him, wrapped her arms around him and held him tight. It was not so much for support as it was to assure him that she was there for him. the vision really worried her as it seemed to last longer than any of the others.

After a few seconds, Matt straightened up and took in a deep breath as he looked up at the sky. Sweat was running down his face and his heart was pounding rapidly. It took him several minutes before he regained his composure completely.

"Are you all right?" she asked as she continued to hold him.

He looked down at her and forced a slight smile. "I think so," he replied.

"You want to sit back down for awhile before we go?"

"No, just give me another minute or so," he said as he wrapped his arms around her.

"You want to tell me about it?"

Becky's mind was filled with confusion. She wanted him to share himself with her, but at the same time she was afraid of what he might tell her.

"I entered an office, the same office that I told you about yesterday. Anyway, the woman that was always yelling at me was sitting behind the desk. She began yelling at me again. It was about not giving her enough money to live on, and that I should sell the business before it went under if I couldn't pay her more. She seemed very upset.

"The other woman came into the room, or office, and was yelled at, too. The woman demanding the money was calling the other woman nasty names.

"I still don't know what it all means," he said as he looked down at Becky.

Becky could see the confusion in his eyes. She wanted to keep him with her, but to keep him from finding out who he was and where he was from would be selfish. She understood that if they were going to have any chance to build a life together, she was going to have to help him find out about himself. That meant letting him go. There was no doubt in her mind that she might lose him to another, but that was the risk she would have to take. She had no choice. If she did not help him find his past, she would never have him completely.

"I think we should go back to the house and give the sheriff a call. Maybe, he has found out who you are and where you belong," she blurted out without giving it any further thought.

Her suggestion instantly grated on her mind. She wanted to think that he belonged here, with her. It did not matter what his past was, she wanted to be with him.

Matt thought about what she had said, too. Deep down he knew that he lived somewhere else and that he had a life somewhere else, but he liked to think that he really did belong here with Becky. Right now, this was the only life he knew, and it seemed to fit him very well. He understood what she was getting at, and that she was right. It would be impossible for him to give himself to her completely until he knew about his past.

"You're right," he agreed with a note of disappointment.

He took his arms from around her, and she stepped away from him. He picked up the backpack and followed her as she turned and began making her way down a narrow trail that led them back to the house. It would be slow going, but that was not all bad. It gave him time to think.

Becky was deep in her own thoughts. She had a difficult time keeping tears from welling up in her eyes since she was so sure that once they got back to the house he would leave her, forever.

In an effort to console herself, she tried to think of last night and earlier that morning. Their time together had been filled with love, desire and passion. All the things she had dreamed of when she found her one true love. If she lost him forever, she would still have that time to remember. It was of little consolation, but it was better than nothing at all.

As they came out of the woods and walked toward the house, they heard voices around in front of the house. They walked around to the front of the house and found Sam and the sheriff sitting on the front porch.

Becky's heart fell as soon as she saw the sheriff. It was clear to her that she was not going to be able to spend the rest of the day with Matt. Their time together was over.

"Hi," Sam said as they came around the corner.

"Hi, Daddy," Becky replied quietly.

"Hi, Sheriff Stevens," she said trying very hard not to show her disappointment.

Matt did not say anything. He simply looked from Sam to the sheriff.

Sheriff Stevens watched Matt as he stood back a little. He knew why Becky and Matt had gone up on the ridge and he wondered if Matt had learned anything about himself.

Sam looked over at the sheriff, then at his daughter. "Honey, why don't you come inside? I think Sheriff Stevens would like to have a talk with our guest, alone."

Becky looked from Matt to the sheriff, then back to Matt. She wondered what he could have to say that they did not want her to hear. It was clear to everyone around that she did not want to leave him now. She hoped that Matt would ask her to stay.

"It's all right. I don't think I have anything to hide. Whatever you have to say to me will be just as much news to me as it will be to her or anyone else."

"Well, all right," the sheriff replied. "But you might want to sit down."

The sheriff waited for Becky and Matt to sit down on the porch swing before he began. "Does the name 'Matthew Steward' mean anything to you?"

"I saw it in one of my visions. Am I Matthew Steward?"

"Yes. Your name is Matthew Steward and you are thirty-two years old. You were married once, but you have been divorced for the past two and a half years. You have no children."

Matt listened very carefully to what he was being told. It was a relief to him to find out that he was not married. He could tell by the look on Becky's face and her squeezing of his hand that she was relieved, too.

The sheriff continued, "You own a small aviation business in Columbus, Ohio. It was not doing very well. You flew to Richmond,

Virginia, to meet with some businessmen. You made a deal with an aviation company there that could put your company back on its feet.

"It seems that when you left Richmond, you ran into a storm and crashed up on the ridge. That just about covers it. The rest you already know."

Matt took a few minutes to absorb everything that he had been told. It seemed strange that his whole life, all thirty-two years, could be wrapped up in such a short report from some county sheriff.

He turned and looked at Becky. It was a relief to him that he was a man free to pursue what he wanted, and he wanted her. Yet, there were still a lot of questions to be answered and things to take care of before he could pursue any other lifestyle.

Becky wanted to throw her arms around him and hold onto him, but the look in his eyes told her that it was not over, not yet. She quickly realized that there were still a lot of pieces of his past that he would have to know. It was clear to her that he would have to leave her and go back to Columbus to find the answers to his past. It was also clear that nothing was going to be simple for them.

"I'll be going back into town shortly. If you want a ride, you can go with me."

"Thank you, sheriff. I appreciate it."

"Frank, come with me. I could use a cup of coffee," Sam suggested as he glanced at Matt and Becky.

"Oh. Sure thing," Sheriff Stevens replied as he stood up and followed Sam into the house.

Becky stood up and walked over to the porch railing. Leaning against the railing, she looked out toward the paddock. She could not see the paddock because her eyes were full of tears.

Matt stood up and stepped up behind her. He wrapped his arms around her as he leaned down and kissed her lightly on the neck.

"I - - guess - - this is - - it. You're going - - to have to - - leave anyway," she said softly, choking on each word.

"Yes."

He squeezed her in his arms. It was not going to be easy for either of them. He had to return to where he had come from if he was going to clear up his past, but that did not make leaving her any easier.

Becky leaned back against him. She liked being in his arms and being close to him. She could not help but think that it was going to be the last time she would be held by him.

"I'll go into town with you," she said.

"I would rather we say goodbye here."

Becky turned around in his arms and looked up at him as she wrapped her arms around his neck. She pulled him down toward her until their lips met. Pressing hard against him, she kissed him deeply and passionately, almost hoping that her kiss would be enough to change his mind and keep him here.

He held her tightly. He did not want to go any more than she wanted him to go. The woman in his arms was more important than anything to him, but he had to go if he was to be truly free of his past.

Matt pulled back and took in a deep breath. Her kiss had been one that he would not easily forget, nor did he want to forget it.

"I'll be back. I don't know how long it will take to get things cleared up, but I will be back. I promise. Will you wait for me?"

"Yes," she replied as tears began to stream down her face.

"I'll miss you," he said softly as he reached up and tried to wipe away her tears.

"I'll miss you, too."

Matt took his hands from her waist and took hold of her hand. Reluctantly, they walked to the door.

"I'm ready, sheriff," he called through the door.

"I'll be right there."

Becky and Matt walked down off the porch to the sheriff's car. Leaning against the car, they waited for the sheriff.

As soon as the sheriff came out of the house, Becky kissed Matt lightly on the lips. She stepped back as he got into the car with the sheriff. Tears streamed down her face as she watched the car go down the lane, then turn onto the road.

Sam stood on the porch watching his daughter. He wished that there was something that he could do to make it easier for her, to make the pain go away; but he knew that there was nothing he could do for her.

Shortly after the car was out of sight, Becky turned, walked past her father and into the house. She went directly to her bedroom, flopped down across her bed and cried herself to sleep.

CHAPTER SEVENTEEN

The days passed into weeks and Becky had not heard from Matt. She was going through the routine of her day without even noticing, or caring what she was doing. It was hard for her to believe that Matt could forget her so quickly. She certainly could not forget him, not even for a minute.

It was a quiet Saturday morning and Becky was sitting on the porch looking out over the paddock. The weather was beautiful and just right for a horseback ride into the mountains.

Sam was beginning to worry about his daughter. Becky had become withdrawn, and spent a lot of her time just sitting around waiting for Matt to return. She refused to go riding or spend any more time then was necessary with her horses. Sam was growing worried about her and would have called Matt, if he knew where he was, and give him a piece of his mind.

"Honey, why don't we go for a ride?" Sam suggested.

"I don't think so."

"You haven't ridden for over a week. You can't just sit around here and wait for him. He's not coming back."

It was hard for Sam to say that to her, but he had to do something to get her mind on other things.

"He is coming back, I know he is. He promised," she said angrily as she looked up at her father.

The sadness in her eyes pulled at Sam's heart. He hated to see his daughter that way, but there was nothing he could do about it. Reluctantly, he turned and left her alone on the porch.

The morning went by slowly. Every time Sam looked out to check on his daughter, she was sitting on the porch swing just staring at the paddock as if Matt would suddenly appear out there.

After lunch, Becky got up and went out to the barn. She turned out all of the horses except Bessy. She began combing Bessy and as she did, she began to talk to the horse.

"Do you think he will ever come back?"

Tears started to fill her eyes. Hearing her own question seemed to bring the realization to her mind that he might never come back.

"I wouldn't bet my paycheck on it."

The sound of another voice startled Becky. She swung around to see Billy Joe standing in the door with a mean grin on his face. He was the last person she expected to see here, and certainly the last person she wanted to see.

* * * *

Sam stepped out on the porch when he saw a car drive up the lane. He did not recognize the car, or the driver, until the car stopped in front of the house. He stepped down off the porch as the driver got out of the car.

"I was beginning to think that you were never coming back," Sam said as he stuck his hand out.

"It took me longer then I thought to get things straightened out. I had some business that I had to clean up before I could come back," Matt replied as he shook hands with Sam.

"How long will you be staying?"

"A long time, I hope."

"Good," Sam replied with a smile.

"Is Becky around?"

"She's in the barn."

"Thanks."

Sam smiled as he watched Matt turn and walk quickly toward the barn. It seemed strange for Sam to feel the way he did, but he was sure that everything was going to be all right now that Matt had come back.

* * * *

"What are you doing here?" The tone in her voice made it clear that she did not want to see him.

"I just came over to see you," Billy Joe replied with a grin. "I could have told you that city boy wouldn't come back for you. He was just using you, like all of them."

As Matt approached the barn door, he heard Billy Joe's voice. He ducked to one side and stepped up along side the door to listen.

"He'll be back, he promised. You get out of here before my father sees you. We don't want you around here any more."

Becky turned and stormed out of the barn. In her anger, she did not see Matt leaning against the side of the barn as she hurried by.

Billy Joe followed her out the door. Just as he stepped out of the barn, he saw something out of the corner of his eye. By the time he realized what was happening, it was too late. Matt's hard right fist caught Billy Joe on the side of his jaw. Billy Joe swung around from the impact, slammed up against the barn, then fell hard to the ground.

"I owed you that," Matt said as he watched Billy Joe fall in the dirt.

Becky heard the noise behind her and turned just in time to see Matt standing over Billy Joe. When Matt turned and looked up at her, she stood frozen as if she were seeing a ghost. It was Matt's smile that brought her back to reality. She ran to him, almost knocking him over as she threw her arms around his neck and kissed him hard on the lips.

Sam had been standing on the porch watching what was happening. He had not expected to see Billy Joe, but when he saw what Matt did to him, he decided to stroll down to the barn. He walked past the lovers and looked down at Billy Joe who was trying to get up.

"I think it would be a good idea if you went and found that horse of yours, get on it and get out of here before you get yourself shot. By the way, don't come back or you will get shot. You understand that, boy?" Sam asked, making sure that there would be no mistaking his meaning.

"Yes, sir," Billy Joe replied as he held his jaw.

Billy Joe got up rather slowly. He went back through the barn to where he had left his horse and rode off.

Sam looked over at Becky and Matt. "You two coming up to the house?"

Matt still had Becky in his arms. "I don't think so. I think we will be going for a ride. We have a lot to talk about," Matt said.

"When will you be back?"

"Tomorrow, tomorrow afternoon," Becky added as she smiled up at Matt.

"Oh. Well, maybe, I should pack some food for you."

"Good idea. That would be nice," Matt replied.

It did not take long for them to pack bedding and food for the overnight, and to saddle the horses. They waved goodbye to Sam as they rode side by side down the valley.

"Did you get everything worked out back in Columbus?"

"I have a lot to tell you and something to ask you, but some of it will have to wait until we get up to that little pool again."

Becky's heart jumped with joy to have him back. She was afraid to ask him too much for fear that she would not want to hear his answers. The important thing was that he was here with her now.

"When I got back to Columbus, I found out that I really did own a small aviation company there. I know that I was told that I did, but I wasn't really sure myself until I saw it.

"I also found out who the two women were that I told you about. The loud one was my ex-wife. I made a deal with her that should keep her out of my life forever."

"What kind of a deal?"

"I sold her my company," he said with a big grin.

"You did what?" Becky could not believe what he said.

"Yeah, I sold her my company. Her daddy put up the money for her. For years she had been telling me how to run it, so I figured the best way to get her off my back was to sell it to her. Let her run it her way."

"What are you going to do now?"

"Oh, I'll think of something."

They had come to the place where they had to turn into the woods. It was probably a good thing that they could not ride side by side while they followed the stream. Becky was wondering what he had in mind. She thought it would be nice if he could stay around here, but he was not a farmer and he had just learned to ride a horse. But that did not matter, she would go wherever he wanted to go just as long as she was with him.

Once again they broke out of the trees into the clearing. They pulled up and dismounted. As they removed the saddlebags and bedding from the horses, Matt looked around. The only sound was that of the slight rustle of the leaves in the breeze and the splashing of the water falling into the crystal clear pool.

Matt dropped the bedding near the fire pit he had built the last time they were here. He removed the saddle from his horse and set it on the ground next to the bedding.

Becky dropped her saddle next to his and turned her horse loose. She watched the horses for a minute or so while they wandered off a little way to graze.

"Okay, we're here," she said expecting him to continue telling her what happened while he was away.

Matt stepped up to her, reached out and put his hands on her waist. As she reached up and put her hands on his shoulders, he pulled her up against him. He leaned down to her and kissed her.

Becky could not help herself, nor did she want to. She melted in his arms and held him tightly. All she could think of was that he was back. She once again felt whole and alive.

Matt released her and motioned for her to sit down on the ground. He sat down beside her and leaned back against one of the saddles.

"You asked me what I am going to do now that I sold my business? I discovered something while I was on your father's farm."

"What was that?"

"I discovered that I don't want to do what I've done in the past. I found something that made me feel good inside, and that's what I want to do."

"What?" she asked, anxious to find out what he was trying to tell her.

"I want to live on a farm and raise horses."

"You're kidding?"

"No."

"You just learned how to ride. You don't know anything about horses, especially raising them."

"True, but you do. You can teach me all about horses."

His response caught Becky by surprise. She sat staring at him. She could not quite figure out what he was saying.

"I want you to marry me. Together, we'll raise horses, and maybe a few kids," he said softly.

Becky hesitated for only a second before she reached over and threw her arms around his neck. The sudden movement pushed Matt off balance, and she rolled over on top of him. She pressed her lips hard against his in a long, deep, passionate kiss. When she rose up, she looked down at him.

"I take it that means 'Yes'," Matt said with a grin.

"Yes, yes, yes."

"Good, because now I won't have to throw you off my property."

Becky wasn't sure that she had heard him correctly.

"What did you say?"

"Does this property belong to your father?"

"Well, no," she replied quietly.

"You're right. It belongs to the farm just to the south of your father's place."

"That's right."

"Then it belongs to us, or at least it will once we sign all the papers. I made an offer on it and it was accepted."

"You're kidding?" she asked excitedly.

"No. It will be our new home, unless you don't want to live here."

"No. I love it here."

Matt slid his hands up behind her head and drew her back down to him. As their lips met, Matt held her tightly, savoring the warmth of her kiss and the feel of her body over him.

Matt rolled over and laid Becky down next to him. Propping his head up in his hand, he looked down at her. There was a warm glow on her face and the sun sparkled in her eyes.

"How about a swim before dinner?"

"We didn't bring our swimsuits," she replied playfully.

"Do we need them?"

"No," she answered as she pulled him down over her and kissed him again.